A CITY BURNING

A CITY BURNING

ANGELA GRAHAM

Seren is the book imprint of
Poetry Wales Press Ltd,
Suite 6, 4 Derwen Road, Bridgend, Wales, CF31 1LH

www.serenbooks.com
facebook.com/SerenBooks
Twitter: @SerenBooks

ISBN: 9781781725917
Ebook: 9781781725924

A CIP record for this title is available from the British Library.

The publisher acknowledges the financial assistance
of the Welsh Books Council.

Cover photography by John Geraint

Printed by Bell & Bain, Glasgow.

CONTENTS

The Road	7
Life-Task	10
Snapshot	15
All Through The Night	20
Above It All	26
Acting Abby	41
Impresario	47
The Triumph	54
Witness	59
Intimacy	65
Repair	69
An Ulster Psyche	79
Mercy	84
Kinship	103
Saint	112
Coasteering	120
Saltem	127
Resistance	132
The Sea Hospital	140
Through Bushes And Through Briars	146
Coward	152
Safety First	165
The Scale	170
Pattern	175
Sugared Almonds	177
Amnesty	184
Acknowledgements	194
Author Note	197

THE ROAD

I made a film about it. Much later. I re-created it. Look. Here. See? A static shot. A frame empty of people. We are at the dark end of a narrow, short hallway. The sun hits our two-up, two-down at the front most of the day, and in it reaches but it can't quite stretch to this passage-end and stairs' foot, so it's from darkness that the camera looks out into the bright day.

Summer outside. Summer 1969. Belfast. East Belfast, where ninety-six per cent of the inhabitants are Protestant and my family are not among that number.

Ahead there is a tiny vestibule and the heavy front door is opened back against its wall. You can see the straight path outside: a chequer-work of black and ox-blood tiles, three strides long; a hip-high wall of smooth-faced red brick is tight against its left side; it ends at a mustard-yellow wooden gate. The matching terrace of houses opposite stands very close and towers in shadow.

Imagine, in that doorway, the back of a tall woman. She's on the threshold, arrested in the act of sweeping the first yard of path outside the door. Her right hand is at the top of the long brush-handle. Another woman, beyond the gate, has stopped and is speaking to her, to my mother. It's a woman who lives in our street but someone we barely know. She has never stopped before. She's on her way somewhere, as she has a coat on and a hat. I see my mother straighten up and the brush-head rise to a standstill, her right hand perched at shoulder-level. The bevelled head of the brush-shaft nestles into the socket of her palm.

What does this neighbour-stranger want?

My mother, stalwart at the door, waits. The woman looks anxious. I move forward, just a little, so I can hear. I am twelve. All the children are being kept indoors, for fear. The woman glances back up the street, the way she has come and then ahead. She'll have seen the main road from where she stands and how empty it is, no passing cars, though it's only early on an August mid-week evening. She'll have known her voice would carry and be heard. I know something's going on. The woman is weak, hovering nervously like that outside our gate. She says – she whines – "Oh, this is awful. Terrible. Things were all right before, weren't they? Before all this began."

My mother would have assured her in some facile way, brushing again, moving the dust towards the gate. But I knew the truth. My mother too.

Have you ever heard thrones fall? When the mighty are cast down, the thrones topple in their wake. They tumble, from an infinite height, colliding and hitting off each other in an ugly way. It should be thrilling and yet there is no sound, like a silent film. For how could there be sound? It is a soundless fall – or sounds like awe, and awe is a soundless thing.

I feel as though I am deep inside a passage tomb, in a chamber that waits and waits (while somewhere that fall unspools) for the moment when the times come right and the sun steps to its vantage-point and shafts the hall, striking the core with light. Then! Then there's a bark of laughter in the dark. A whoop that echoes off the walls.

The words leapt inside me, licking the walls like flames: *Things were not all right.*

What did she want us to say, that woman? Did she want us to tell her, *You have no guilt. We'll be more than kind, now that our day has come. We'll see you right.*

She moved on. I went into the street. The sky, where the sunset should have been, was a weird orange-rose colour and a tree of smoke had risen, was rising, crawling upward, against it. Something huge was burning – the city west of us.

Sirens trailed their tales across the evening air – *hurry – help me – save me – stop me.* Each July the Twelfth I'd be kept indoors as the bonfires at every junction blazed to keep us Catholics down. But what's afire now? Let them – let *them* taste fear for a change.

There's another angle I never captured.

A first, and then a second, soldier was shot when I was fourteen. When I heard that three had been killed together I felt a spurt of reasonable delight. Their loss not ours. I was again in the house when I heard. I was standing in the living-room. The door to the hallway was open. Its wall, that I could see ahead of me, was papered in white embossed stripes and the masterful sun, thrusting in and along, made the contours bold in profile.

By hedges, then, I heard, on the radio news. Sparse March hedges and roadside whins, I imagined, on a cold brae, and spiteful sleet on their gullible teenage skin. A pint glass glinting in the ditch. Their trousers down.

If I'd touched it, the wallpaper would have been warm. Warm to the touch.

It couldn't be right to be glad.

I stepped into a humble road, of cheap black tar, hedged either side.

A child can choose.

LIFE-TASK

It was a very still day. I can only say as I remember and I remember how the air was on the verge of something. We stood under a dome of cloud, whitish, like a plaster ceiling. We stood with this vast lid above us. The railway tracks insisted on the distance, the far distance over the surface of Europe, the distance between them and us. We had seen the tracks as black lines on the maps we had worried over so often. The lines entered and left the dots of cities, and now the train was coming back towards us, entering and leaving city – village – tunnel. We could imagine that train but not the people in it, not as they were now. We knew they would have changed.

I had no one to imagine in particular. Mine were lost early in the war. I was waiting at the station because I couldn't not be there. They all had to have a homecoming even if it wasn't my home any of them were coming to.

Yes, the air was about to do something. It was too still. Maybe the force of all those eyes – straining to see the engine breach the bend of track far off – maybe they had paralyzed it, as someone entering a room freezes at the many gazes turned in his direction. The air had been struck into immobility.

We just are, aren't we, on a normal day? We go about our business not thinking of the air we move through and it moves around us, as the wind and weather. We battle on. But here, today, the air held its breath and I knew suddenly that the air was just like those eyes, those eyes that feel a prickle in the duct as tears gather but can't fall. Just can't. Why cry? These were the lucky ones, the ones coming back.

Backs I mostly saw, turned away from me, looking along the tracks. There was an uncertainty about everything. The tone wasn't right. Coloured bunting had been strung along the station buildings but it did nothing in the stricken atmosphere. Some people wore their best – what they still had of it. Some were in their brightest colours which somehow seemed not bright enough – a sort of defeated gaiety. Others wore black. They had lost, you see, and had to signal that, even to the ones who had made it through.

Not much talk. Speculation had run dry. People checked and re-checked the official letter received, giving the train number, the passenger's name – the crucial name – every detail verified again and again. "Yes, it's our Taddeo. Taddeo Felipepe. See here." A note of pride in that, the only Felipepe in town. *Foolish*, I remember thinking! *Do you think he cares? After what he's seen?*

Just as I was deliberately releasing my fingers from the fist they'd crumpled into, I felt that uncanny tremble, building to a tremor, which runs through iron rails and buds into view as a tiny, dull mirage far off. Instantly everyone moved. The Stationmaster emerged. He had been hiding, I suspected, because he couldn't work out what note to strike with this crowd. Banter or officiousness were his usual options and even he knew something unique was called for. He held sheets of names. People watched him carefully as if his list guaranteed a safe delivery. Everyone whose name was on that list was safe. Life could return to normal once this train emptied itself at our platform and, as it drew out and away, we could turn our backs on it and go home.

The station-master's appearance released his staff into the crowd. Poor men. They could only pace the platform-edge uneasily. Weren't they also expecting a brother, a son or a friend?

Some nurses and nuns moved a little forward in readiness though we'd been told that these were walking wounded. Yes, if they had survived the prison camps and were in this first batch of returnees they'd have to be fairly mobile.

The town band shuffled up. The mayor patted his sash and consulted his notes one last time. A worried man. Work for amputees? Shell-shock victims hanging around the piazzas like after the Great War, arousing disgust and pity? He couldn't guess. Too early. And the partisans to deal with, for whom these veterans were despicable. Such a settling of scores to come, not least for his own allegiances. And his wife here in a fur coat!

The locomotive drew closer and bigger and slid to a clanking stop, its great reptilian tail behind it. I felt an irrational fear that it would lurch up over the platform that kept it corralled on its track and mount towards us, hissing and snorting. The band blared out. People sought a focus, left and right, but nothing happened. No door swung wide. The crowd recoiled slightly. Why did none of the passengers come to the windows? Then a young woman dashed forward, calling a name. A porter intercepted her and, just as everyone watched her struggle, a figure appeared on the open steps of the foremost carriage. There was a blotch of colours on his breast. He paused, scanning the scene from this vantage-point and everyone turned towards him, even the struggling pair. He had shrunk inside his uniform but we recognised him. Our hero.

He looked pained. His handsome face tightened. He raised his hand – to salute, I expected – but before the gesture was complete he stopped and his hand seemed to brush aside a veil. The mountains! He could see them beyond the town. Of course. His hand snapped into a salute as he looked at our mountains. Our beautiful mountains. We felt their beauty as our own. He looked at them, at us, and his look released us. A groan rose from the crowd, then a wailing, shouts, and names one after the other as people surged towards the train, banging on the carriage windows and on the sides of the wagons that made up the bulk of it. Why was no one coming out? He made a gesture to the Stationmaster who blew his whistle in response.

They came! Hesitantly, pale, strained, keyed-up; some looking anxious, some blank... What chaos! What clutching and touching and inspecting and stumbling. I saw a man fall to his knees in front of his son. I heard a farmer say to his brother, "You look..." The brother held up the cuff of an armless sleeve. The farmer sighed, then said wryly, "You never were much good for a day's work." The general's wife stood rigid in front of him, staring at his coloured decorations. Then she started to cry and he stepped towards her and embraced her, comforting her. He looked suddenly immensely weary, like a man taking on a burden.

The mayor never gave his speech. The important things were getting said without him. I watched as one reclamation after another took place. Everyone wanted to get away with their precious cargo as soon as possible. The band gave up. The platform emptied. Only one woman was left. She was not yet thirty, pretty and slight, trying hard to keep calm despite the fear rising in her as she was gradually marooned. She gripped her letter as she waited and looked at it from time to time. The Stationmaster avoided her but at last she confronted him up by the head of the train. He shrugged. I couldn't hear what he said. Shiftily, he pointed her to the rear and I knew he thought it was hopeless. As he passed me, I heard him confirm the train number dully. Yes, the right train and date. He disappeared into his office and closed the door on the man who hadn't come back.

She ran, as though the Stationmaster was an oracle, down the empty platform. I moved far enough to watch. She reached the very last truck just as its door was pushed heavily back. A soldier looked out. Not hers, evidently, for she immediately craned past him. He shoved the door further and a second soldier appeared. They seemed annoyed and embarrassed. One of them jumped down onto the platform, ignoring her roughly. He raised his arms above his head and I saw him grip the handles of a stretcher. His colleague shouted at her to get back as they lowered a body onto the platform. A greatcoat slid off, followed by a blanket. The soldiers both hesitated, then walked away, pulling out cigarettes. One of them glanced back briefly and his resentment was clear.

She stood, looking down. Her gaze moved the length of the stretcher and back. She made a sound. That's all I can say. The body on the stretcher had no arms and no legs and the face was busted. I think he knew she was there, precisely because he kept his face turned away from her. He wasn't even in uniform but in a dirty nightshirt. He looked grotesque and ridiculous and he stank. She dropped her letter and her bag and stood with her empty hands held out a little from her body, getting the measure of him. She whispered his name, then again, as he didn't react. She knelt beside him. "It's me," she said. Nothing. Leaning closer, she said, "It's you." He opened his eyes but didn't turn to her. "It's you," she repeated and she kept saying this till he moved his battered head to meet her gaze. What a lucky man. No one had ever looked at me with such love. I found my own eyes wet. She put her lips to his ruined face then leapt to her feet and bawled down the platform, "Come back here! Come back! Help me bring my husband home, you bastards!"

The soldiers hurried towards her and she left the station ahead of them, like a queen, with her consort carried behind her.

I want to be seen like he was. That was my thought. I looked at the ugly train, the tawdry bunting, the station's vacancy. How would she see them? I set myself to learn.

SNAPSHOT

Oh, this would make Richard's day; make his day, she thought. Myrtle stiffened in the car seat, longing to be invisible – no, to be *not here*. "Not here," she begged him silently, as though her plea would reach him through the windscreen as he stood by the front bumper, looking grimly down at the number plate.

The couple whose car, in backing up to pull out, had lightly touched the front of Richard's, looked perplexed as they stood by their bumper. The man – the husband, she supposed – had apologized readily, saying that despite the relentless holiday traffic and the pressure on the roadside parking spaces he should have been able to get out ok. It was a rare mistake on his part, he added and she thought he did look annoyed – at himself. The July traffic processed doggedly past them, between the palisade of seafront shops and the meagre promenade.

Myrtle turned towards the sea. That's why they had parked here, after all: to see the sea. Richard, she felt, respected the sea without being interested in it. It was large and powerful and had its job to do but he was a countryman and liked firm ground under his feet. He didn't like beaches.

There the sea was, where it always was, amazingly close to the line of parked cars, the pedestrian crossing, the rubbish bins, ice cream parlour, newsagent's festooned with beach balls and coloured tat, the home bakery and the butcher's shop. Nothing could take away from the flamboyance of the view. This was an ocean, more than a sea – touched by the Atlantic – and daily it threw together spectacular displays of sunshafts and cloudbanks regardless of whether anyone watching deserved them. A yellowish light pushed against grey masses of cloud. To the west, the jewel-green slopes of the Free State − it too so startlingly close − flickered, now bright, now shaded, as the sun picked out one field or another. Republic of Ireland, that's what people called it these days. The sea, closer in to shore, heaved. She thought of a man turning over under blankets, giving you the cold shoulder, again and again.

She looked back. Had Richard said anything? No. The silent treatment. He bent down, slowly inclining his great height, and scrutinised the car. She knew what would happen. The man, unnerved by the prolonged silence, would incriminate himself.

"I don't think there's any damage," he said rather meekly. No response from Richard but a continued silent inspection. "I've said it was my fault," the man went on, "but I can't see any mark."

She saw Richard's left hand, flat on the silver-grey car bonnet which was little different in colour to his head of thick hair that was level with the car mascot. Seventy and not a hint of the aches and pains of age. She knew he was remarkable and remarks were often made at his stately vigour, his upright presence. He'd pretend not to credit them. The hand − a massive hand − tensed on the bonnet as he levered himself back up.

"Can you see anything?" the man asked.

His voice was Welsh, she realised with some surprise. You didn't meet Welsh people. Not here on the north Antrim coast. On holiday, probably. Then, a little muffled by the windscreen, she heard the woman say, "I can't see anything. There's no damage, I'd say." She, now, was from the North – Belfast − by the sound of her. "Wouldn't you think?" she added firmly.

"Some damage doesn't show till later," Richard said, shaking his head judiciously. He patted the car. "She's just out of the show-room. I've had her but two days."

"Two days. Yes," said the man, somewhat helplessly.

"She's just out of the showroom," Richard repeated, looking along the whole length of the car.

"I can see why you'd be concerned but luckily there doesn't seem to be a mark on her... on the car."

As Myrtle could have predicted, at this, Richard pursed his lips and drew himself up. This wouldn't do. "Your name and registration, sir."

The woman looked angry.

"Ah, yes, of course," the man said. "I could write the reg. down but I don't have a...."

Richard solemnly opened his car door and took his time leaning across Myrtle to open the glove compartment and take out a pen and a notebook. She might as well not have been there. Back outside he noted down the numbers, his shoulders squared, his brow stern. Passers-by had begun to notice him.

"Your name, sir." Not a question. An indictment.

The Welshman said something with a lot of 'ell' sounds that ended in 'Griffiths'.

Richard's pen hesitated.

"Double ell, Y, W..." the Welshman said carefully.

"Double ell," Richard echoed. The laborious name-spelling went on. The woman glared in the background till Myrtle saw her suddenly re-focus on Richard and she gave a sneering, putting-two-and-two-together smile. Once addresses had been exchanged Richard closed the notebook and fitted its elastic strap across it.

"And your name, sir?" the Welshman asked, respectfully.

The woman gave a quick, incredulous shake of the head and raised her eyes to heaven.

"Meikle. Richard Meikle. Magherabwee House, Kildart."

Uncertainly the Welshman said, "Meek...?"

"Meikle," the woman said aggressively. "M,E,I,K,L,E. A good Ulster name, that." The 'that' came out like a slap.

Richard turned away from her and addressed the man. "She's brand new," he said ponderously, his hand stroking the car's shining flank. He gave the husband a nod, enlisting him, man-to-man, against the woman.

"Yes, sir," said the Welshman, uneasy at his wife's belligerence.

Suddenly she whipped out a mobile phone, held it up towards the car's bumper and clicked. She crouched quickly and clicked again, closer. Without warning, she stood and aimed the camera at the windscreen. Click! She stepped back and got the Welshman and Richard. She moved methodically around the car, taking shots as she went. Myrtle was appalled. It wasn't happening! It couldn't.

Richard waved his arms and shouted, "You stop that this instant!"

"Why?" she laughed.

"Because I say so!"

She raised the phone and captured him in his outrage. He reached for her but she darted round to the other side of the car. By now, people were pointing and gawping and the traffic had slowed to get a look.

"A crime, is it? You'd know, I guess."

Myrtle did not turn to see what was happening behind her. She imagined Richard swelling, sweating. The woman walked by the side window.

"You'll be wanting the evidence," the woman said jeeringly to him. "So will we. Don't worry. We know where you live...." She paused, then, with relish, she added emphatically, and loudly enough for the street to hear, 'Dick!'"

There was laughter from the bystanders and some amused shock.

The woman called to her husband, who looked stunned. He leapt into the driver's seat. As the woman opened the passenger door she was already throwing her husband's deferential 'Sir' mockingly back at him. "You're not in Wales now!"

Richard got into his driving seat and the inevitable awfulness followed.

A week later, an envelope arrived with a Welsh postmark. Richard was annoyed by the contents. When he went with his newspaper to the toilet she took from the envelope several photographs: details of the car, including Richard and the Welshman. Among them was a snapshot of the hood and windscreen and there, to one side, she saw herself: a woman in her sixties, a functional hairdo, maroon clothes, and an expressionless face. Myrtle was shocked. Amidst all that carry-on, with all the fearful turmoil she'd been feeling inside, she had looked like that? Stolid and unmoved. Blank.

A note was signed Siobhán Griffiths. A Catholic, then. She was bound to see Richard in a certain light: the oppressor, the righteous bully asserting a waning authority.

She looked at a snap of Richard. She looked at herself.

Some damage doesn't show till later.

Forty-two years.

But for it not to show at all...!

She rehearsed a word to the Richard in the photo. Then she said it aloud. "Dick," she said. "Dick. Dick. Dick!" She caught her reflection in the act of saying it. Her teeth were bared.

ALL THROUGH THE NIGHT

I look back now with a kind of dread, yet dread is about the future, about what's going to happen, not what has already happened. So I dread...? The memory of pain.

I never thought of myself as a man given to gestures. Imagination I do have, but I tend to keep it to myself.

I remember the road: the little road under the starlight that summer. It was the year Mam and Dad sold the farm. I didn't want it. They kept the farmhouse and the little *bwthyn* that had been the kernel of the homestead. You and I had used it for years already for holidays with the kids. They loved its thick walls and deep window-ledges.

At *Clogwyn Uchel*, on the very edge of Wales, the roads are dark (some of them are tracks, really) and the stars sort of spread themselves out overhead, display themselves, with a careless glamour; or like something much more homely, like sugar spilt across a slate, but up there, up above. A sprinkling of sugar overhead. Very confusing if you thought about it too much. And higher into the sky – it's hard to describe! – there's a hazy cloud of them. Growing up at *Clogwyn Uchel* and I never bothered to learn much about them. Anyway, the stars do what they do whether we notice them or not. They're not waiting for our attention.

On a clear night like that one they shed enough light to see your way and the chalky ground of the lane helps. It's a glimmering path up to the *bwthyn*, reflecting light from far, far above. Sometimes it even seems to me as though a bit of the sky has dropped to earth because the little white stones are like a rough and tumble Milky Way between the hedges.

You walked ahead of me, Mari. Blindly, I thought. Or like someone who'd been dazzled by something. Your feet took you.

Your mind? Numbed.

Probably. We all have to do so much guess-work about each other! What is she feeling? What will she do next? What does she want?

"Do you love him?" I called out. But you didn't stop, or look back, or speak. I'm sure you heard me. You went on, into the little house.

I couldn't. I walked around it to where the sea suddenly presents itself. A shock! Always. Always that shiver at finding yourself on the edge of a cliff. Acres of water ahead in a dark mass. The endlessness of the sea. It doesn't stop. It goes about its business, rushing and crushing, floating boats, flexing itself. That night it was shuddering.

The stars. Some flung themselves down the sky. Mad bastards. Most looked on in a dignified way, blinking mildly at this recklessness. And I thought of the song. Its beautiful tune.

Holl amrantau'r sêr ddywedant
Ar hyd y nos.

Ar hyd y nos. All through the night.

Nothing like the crappy English version. Sickly-sweet, that. And boring. "Soft the drowsy hours are creeping... visions of delight revealing... hill and vale in slumber steeping". And the stars don't get a look-in! Not a mention. You pointed that out to me. When you were learning Welsh. "How come...?" you asked. You were always asking that. "Why is the verb here? Why do I have to say...?" Whatever.

And I'd say, "It just is, Mari. I don't know why. Ask your teacher, *cariad*. Gwyn knows all that stuff."

Yes, he did, didn't he? *Holl amrantau'r sêr... amrantau* – such a great-sounding word for such a workaday bit of us: our eyelids. "All the eyelids of the stars are saying". Eyelids speak? Oh, yes. They shield or conceal. They widen to reveal.

Dyma'r ffordd i fro gogoniant.

"This is the way to the land of glory. All through the night. *"* Go on, stars, I remember thinking that night, as I stood with them all above me, show us the way.

Oh, I closed my eyes then, I did. Because I was lost.

That stuff from the bible swam into my head:

Pan edrychwyf ar y nefoedd, gwaith dy fysedd....

"When I consider thy heavens, the work of thy fingers...." How does it go? "The stars which thou hast ordained.... What is man, that thou art mindful of him?... a little lower than the angels... crowned with glory and honour...."

Shit. Nothing like a chapel upbringing for loading you with stuff that makes you feel like shit in comparison. Sunday School set pieces. So beautiful the pictures in your head. No Special Effects needed. Just the words. You can see it happening: the stars being set in place one by one, like diamonds. And look at them up there, murmuring cheerfully to one another, "Here we are! Just where we should be. But we'll cast ourselves from heaven in an instant. Give the word. No problem."

But me? I was bloody lost. Lost.

We'd gone walking on the beach, earlier, you and me, between the pebbly border of the sea and the wrack and old bits of driftwood and plastic oddments that stack up high against the cliff. Between that stony fringe – it always hurt my feet as a child; I'd teeter across it, complaining, excited at my own bravery, me versus the chilly little waves; like someone walking over hot coals, I'd think, secretly proud (look at me, Mam! Dad!) − between those stones and the cliff there's a narrow crescent of smooth beige sand. It doesn't change. Same for our kids as it had been for me. You and I walked along it towards the setting sun but you wouldn't look at me and couldn't speak. Couldn't, I say, because you just shook your head sadly at every question.

We ended up just walking. I found myself scrutinising the sun's angle − how the low shafts of sun hit the beach − and how they struck stars out of the damp sand: tiny mica fragments that glinted ahead of every step I took. Walking on a constellation. Yes, I could think a thought like that even with all that was going on because that's the kind of mind I've got. I don't like misery. I sheer off it. Think of something else! Cheer up! It'll never happen.

But that night? Not a single bloody joke.

So later, when I stood out there in the darkness in front of the *bwthyn*, I looked up at the stars and I thought: we're surrounded; we haven't a chance. Stars above us. Stars below us. And we're stuck in the middle. The shit in the sandwich. Who'd want to stay here? Why would you stay?

And then, I knew you were behind me. I felt you. You were still inside, mind; behind me, looking out through the window of the dark house; looking out at the same pointlessly lovely display, the Plough and all the other things we don't know the names of, you and me.

And I was desperate and I suppose it was so I wouldn't cry that I did it. I started to sing. Was I showing you I didn't care? Big man. Mad man to *sing* at a time like that!

Golau arall yw tywyllwch,

I arddangos gwir brydferthwch,

"Darkness is another type of light" − to show us true beauty, the beauty of "the family of the heavens", the stars, "in silence, all through the night".

And I went on, louder; that tune rising, like a wave rolling up to its crest,

Nos yw henaint pan ddaw cystudd

"Night is old age". That's "when trouble hits us"; really hits us. Hits us when we're least able for it; gets us in an armlock and grinds us down, Mam and Dad.

And the tune sinks gradually, gradually, into calm and quiet, like a wave relaxing. Dark night is coming, it tells us; our youth is dead. I couldn't roll with the blows so well. I was getting the measure of myself a bit, frankly: a man in my middle years; nothing special.

Ond i harddu dyn a'i hwyrddydd

"But to make ourselves and our day's end beautiful…" – to have something (at least something) to hold on to – "let's put our fragile lights together… All through the night".

I couldn't help it. I couldn't, couldn't help it. I just cried.

I'd thought you'd always be there, see. *Ar hyd y nos.*

I stood out there and I cried. And I knew you were watching me. And I couldn't stop.

Pity, was it, that made you stay that night? The next morning the sky was like the inside of a sea shell, pearly pink and white. The stars had gone. We were still there.

Later, much later, you told me that when you'd looked out you'd thought, *My husband, singing in the darkness*. I had surprised you. You saw me silhouetted against the sky while a star dropped gracefully across it, beyond me, and you thought: *Have I just watched the last moment of something that's millions of years old?* You saw, you told me – as though it were really there – the white heart of a November bonfire, the children's figures scampering, black, against it; bunches of sparks dancing up above the orange flames; and one particular spark, floating, higher and higher, wavering, till it expired, gently, and as silently as a shooting star.

And, there I was, one particular man. As though I'd come into focus again. And you chose. Because however hard things had become we had created a life together. Something real. Something real as a mad bastard singing on a cliff-top. You chose me. Just for tonight, you told me you remembered thinking; we'll see about tomorrow.

Our fragile lights. Together. We do what we can, aye. Our lives are brief and *Hir yw'r nos.* Night is long.

And so, today, I've chosen: your name, with stars above and stars below. We walk on stars, with stars high overhead but life is in the middle, *pan ddaw cystudd, cariad.* A rough road, my love.

The mason's asked me why I have him carving stars on your stone. I'll tell him, but everyone else, as time goes by, will have to work it out for themselves.

ABOVE IT ALL

A little red car darted forward from a junction. It shot into a stream of traffic jetting across a piazza and sped along a boulevard but, approaching the next crossroads it was seen to hesitate, signal left, then right, then, on the brink of commitment, it lurched forward, just escaping collision with a tourist bus to the side and a van in front. Horns and a klaxon and protesting, screeching brakes clamoured in the car's wake as it disappeared into the melée of Rome's summer morning traffic. In it were three priests: two of them young.

"Are you a stupid man, Liam?" asked O'Reilly, the old one, from the front passenger seat. "Are you a man, now, who makes bad decisions under pressure, would you say?" Liam gripped the steering-wheel even tighter and even more tightly gritted his teeth, telling himself not to answer, not to rise to the bait. He hated O'Reilly. He wanted to swat him out of existence with the back of his hand like the whining irritant he was. "I always heard you were a great man for the technicalities of life," O'Reilly went on. "Isn't that so, Donal?" he added, tilting his chin towards the back-seat passenger but keeping his eyes on the road ahead.

Liam glanced into the mirror. Donal's dark eyes met his there sympathetically, as he replied, deflecting their superior's attention, "More the technologies in Liam's case, Father. As for the technicalities, you yourself are known as being a stickler for them in your own work."

"Yes, in texts, yes. But when it comes to machinery...." He sniffed. "I dare say it's a talent. One about which I must needs be modest."

He expected, and was provided with, a contradictory murmur from Donal. Liam flashed an angry look via the mirror and received an apologetic, good-humoured wink in return. Donal was hunched forward because the back seat was cramped and he was a burly man, broad-shouldered, with big country-man's hands. His knees were pressed against the seats in front.

"Have you heard from the publishers?" Donal asked O'Reilly. "Have they a date yet?"

"They have. I'm to choose between three dates. They're being very obliging, I must say. 'Totally at your convenience, Monsignor O'Reilly,' they said." His complacent smile stretched his spare, pasty skin more tautly over his skull.

No doubt, Liam thought, O'Reilly considered his appearance appropriately ascetic. He could glimpse the old man's hands, clasping a briefcase on his lap. They were swollen. Arthritis. Liam felt no sympathy. As O'Reilly talked on, Liam concentrated on getting them to the Vatican, grateful for Donal's deliberate absorption of his tittle-tattle. Donal had the patience for it.

With the car stowed and security clearances done, they followed O'Reilly along a pillared portico. Why couldn't the man just get a taxi, Liam fumed. What were he and Donal doing, trailing in his wake, like ducklings? No, like pages – bridesmaids, even, in their full-length habits! That's all it was: vanity. O'Reilly wouldn't do even a small commission like this one without a little retinue, making a point: "Look how healthy the Order is. We have men to spare for the smallest tasks." That was their function today: walking billboards.

Liam saw, beyond the pillars, up above the balconies and the roof tiles, the sky. It was sharply blue. Someone opened a high window and a pane flashed like a semaphore. He felt himself respond: *What? Up there? Come up there? Above it all! Yes!* He felt a touch on his arm and turned to see Donal looking concerned. Had he groaned aloud? He sighed. "Donal, I don't know what I'd do without you," he muttered. "You're the only sane one of them all."

Ahead of them, O'Reilly announced his business to one of the Swiss Guards at an entrance. Out in the courtyard a troop of his colleagues marched past. Powerfully slender, on their way to some formal occasion, they wore the distinctive, conquistador-style, striped and slashed uniform – blue, orange and yellow – with a scarlet plume waving from their glinting, pointed helmets. How strange, Liam reflected: three men in funereal black – in skirts, basically – and others dressed like peacocks: the flamboyant, martial males. Truly there was a place for everyone in the Roman Catholic Church. The full spectrum.

The tall young man inspecting their credentials was wearing the plain, blue duty uniform and black beret. Liam saw a look pass between the Guard and Donal. Did they know each other? Neither spoke. Did Donal know *everyone*? Liam sometimes thought so. Donal: so quiet, so observant, given to good deeds without fuss. Who knew what he'd done for this man? Liam wouldn't ask because Donal prized discretion. If questioned, his pleasant features would crimson to the roots of his black peasant hair and... 'peasant'? Liam caught the word, displeased with himself. It was true, he knew, that that's how he saw his friend: a big, Irish labouring man, white-skinned and curly-haired, needing to stoop through doorways and manage his great strength in narrow confines when his body might have been easier digging, lifting, striding... But Liam didn't see himself as a labeller; he prided himself on seeing people as individuals. He tossed the peasant-thought from him.

But a holiday memory returned to him: Donal, in a cliff-edge field overlooking the Donegal Atlantic, tossing stones to his brothers from a broken wall, the steady pressure of the sea-wind preventing words; the same wind provoking white wave-caps on the dark, glittering ocean. A glittering day. That's what Liam remembered. Now it occurred to him that that had been Donal in his element.

As the Guard let them pass through the doorway Liam wondered how Donal had disciplined himself to years of study. Perhaps his mind was hungry too? Not as hungry as mine, Liam thought, confident of his own keen intelligence. They had spent part of their novitiate together, then Liam had been loaned to a different province and within the last year they had both been assigned to Rome. Liam felt they got on well. Donal was a good listener.

On that same holiday, he'd been in a rowing-boat with Donal, on a calm day. The boat rocked a little as they let it float, just enough movement to be soothing. Liam lay under the sun, under the blue sky, opening himself to the heat. Sprinklings of light he allowed through his lashes: scintillae. He felt a little spark of pleasure at the exactitude of the word. He had sung, without effort, "*Volare... oh ho; Cantare... oh woh oho; Nel blu dipinto di blu; Felice di stare lassù...*" On he sang, repeating himself at random. *To sing, to fly, in the blue painted blue, happy to stay there on high.* When he'd opened his eyes, Donal was gazing at him in the frankest admiration. Sea-birds glided overhead with masterly ease. Liam had closed his eyes and continued humming, smiling, singing: "*E volavo, volavo felice più in alto del sole... and higher again, while the world bit by bit disappeared far away down below.*" He soared.

On the way back to shore he'd had the oars. Donal had fussed: it was too far, let him take over; no trouble and so on, and Liam, struggling, had persisted, irked that he should be thought incapable. Singing wasn't all he could do!

And now, here they were, years later, fully trained, professed, fledged. Dry feathers, he thought resentfully. Dusty birds.

Voices reached him now from ahead, murmuring in Italian. O'Reilly stopped at an open office door, was greeted from inside and went in, closing the door behind him, abandoning them without explanation. Liam turned to Donal indignantly. Donal raised a hand signalling patience, walked along to the next office and spoke to its occupant. A smart young woman came to the threshold, smiling. She beckoned to Liam as she ushered Donal around a corner, chatting animatedly. Donal did know everyone!

"I never saw her before," Donal insisted simply as they sat at the formica-topped table in a modest kitchen-cum-dining room. The woman had done her best to make them comfortable with coffee and dry little biscuits. Liam was at the head of the table, Donal at its broad side, on a metal chair whose spindly legs squeaked on the terrazzo floor at any movement. Time crawled past. Liam employed it in telling Donal what he thought of O'Reilly and his ilk, and all he stood for: the life-denying, status-seeking, petty-minded, cerebral.... "I hate him!" he said. He felt the pleasure of inserting the scalpel exactly on the puncture point. "His nit-picking, old-womanish ways and his rudeness, and his insinuations. Why doesn't he just *say* things?"

Donal sat in silence, his discomfort evident in his hunched shoulders, his furrowed brow, his eyes that, Liam could swear, had grown even darker. But Liam ignored these signs. Never a bad word about anyone from Donal, he thought irritably, so he said a good few more to compensate. He didn't notice himself leaning forward on his elbows, letting his clenched fist fall heavily onto the table, time and again, in an unconscious act of obliteration. Liam's frustration and grievance absorbed him, exalted him and Donal's very distress excited him. At least it was a reaction!

Suddenly there was a scrape of metal on stone and Liam, startled, felt his descending fist engulfed and arrested between Donal's great hands. "Liam!" Donal said gruffly, urgently; and again, "Liam". Liam felt his fist squeezed tightly and shaken a little. "This," said Donal, "is your heart." As though in a dream, he watched Donal gently prise open his fingers, bend his dark head over Liam's palm and place a kiss right at its core. When Donal looked up at him, Liam read and re-read, in an instant, a message of love, reproach and devotion. He saw his hand still resting between Donal's.

Then there was movement, a terrible clatter of metal, and the chair was falling behind him and he was wiping his hand on his habit and backing away and saying something searing – he could feel it in his mouth – and Donal was infinitely far away, his face signalling emotion which Liam could not bear to decipher.

Liam reached the exit and pummelled the glass panel. He saw the Swiss Guard's face peer through and register that something was amiss. Before the man could raise any alarm, Liam called out, "I'm sick. Let me out!" To his relief, the door opened and the Guard caught him as he stumbled through.

"You look dreadful," the man said and next moment was speaking into a mouthpiece pulled from somewhere inside his uniform while Liam rubbed his upper arm in the wake of his strong grip. "Leave by the way you came in, with your I.D. ready. Take it easy, Father." The Guard's blue eyes were sympathetic but Liam turned away, recalling the look that had passed between this handsome man and Donal. Had he failed to read that right? As he had failed to read Donal?

He hurried out. The crowds in Saint Peter's Square, the honking coaches, the souvenir displays, the guides holding umbrellas aloft to shepherd their charges – he plunged through them all, away down a side street and towards the river. He walked in inner turmoil as he reviewed his whole conception of Donal: that afternoon in the boat; times they'd gone swimming together; confidences he had made; ambitions confided; gestures accepted. He dodged the traffic and crossed the Tiber. He hurried past a couple of blocks and, when he came to an open junction, instinctively veered towards the narrowest of the streets that led off it. How much he had shown Donal and, looking back on it now, how little Donal had ever revealed in return. Till now!

"Are you a stupid man?" he heard O'Reilly's voice. "Would you say you're a man prone to errors of judgement?" He burned with shame. How did it look to men like O'Reilly? To other people? Could they see what he hadn't? Did they think that he...? God! He covered his face with a hand and that slowed him down. He realised that he was being stared at by passers-by.

The street was in shade, being very narrow. It was lined with workshops, of upholsterers and leather-workers – dusty, dry things anyway – yet here and there was a window glinting with niche-market luxuries. It was a very Italian mixture of the homely and the high-end. A bulky man, seated in his open-fronted shop, surrounded by domestic appliances, was eyeing him uncertainly. Liam moved on, though each step was leaden. He replayed the incident in the dining-room. He was... desired? Could what he had thought of as admiration be – his stomach tightened – lust? As quickly as images occurred to him of intimacies with Donal – being looked after during an illness last winter; falling asleep on his shoulder during an endless bus journey; accepting kindnesses (Donal taking the draughty seat, queuing for tickets, forgoing the last of the wine) – he pushed them away. They were tainted.

He stopped. He had come to a halt at a shop window, a single large pane of glass. Behind it were brightly coloured, jumbled things. He stared, unseeing, but he felt. He felt acutely. Humiliated. Deceived. Donal was going to open him up, was he? Free up the tight-fisted, tight- ... ! Liam swerved away from the thought.

The shop doorbell pinged and a man emerged, close enough to touch: a slim, middle-aged Italian in a good suit, smiling. "I see you are very interested, Father. I'm not surprised. A gem. And you spotted it at once. It's only been in the window half an hour and for half that time you've been looking at it. Don't deny it! I was watching you." He held the door open.

Liam entered the shop because that was easier than explaining his behaviour and he could make an excuse after a moment and leave. He didn't even know what he was supposed to be intrigued by. Luckily the man seemed very sure. He motioned to Liam to be seated on an elegant chair at a small, baize-covered table. An antiques shop, Liam realized. He felt totally in the shop owner's hands and would perhaps make a fool of himself so when the man said emphatically, "However, if you will allow me, I will put before you something of even greater interest," he assented at once.

The shop owner switched on a lamp that cast a circle of light onto the table and into it he placed a rectangular object of A4 size. A portrait. It gleamed. It was like nothing precisely that Liam had seen before yet it resembled an icon. A three-quarter-length figure was placed solidly at the centre against a plain gold background. It was a priest, or at least a cleric. He wore a white surplice over a black cassock. His right hand was raised in blessing, his left hand rested on his solar plexus. It *was* like an icon, but the face...! What a beautiful face. In no way abstracted to its essentials as in a true icon, this was the face of a thoroughly observed individual. No one could doubt that whoever had painted this had seen and known the subject: a man aged about thirty, black-haired, strong-shouldered, strong-featured and attractive.

"You see!" the shop owner announced triumphantly. "He smiles and he does not smile. He smiles without smiling. The artist has managed a great thing." He paused. Liam understood that he was being offered the pleasure of stating the obvious. When he didn't – couldn't – the man tapped the table with a finger and said, "He has painted the interior joy – here around the eyes – and in the entire demeanour." Liam nodded readily, because, yes, this priest had a certain quality, something grounded, humane. The shop owner, noting Liam's assent, sat back, pleased. He slid something underneath the painting to prop it up for Liam's inspection. There was no frame and it seemed to be done on card or light wood.

Liam gazed with pleasure, taking in the skilfully rendered details. Here was a real person. Someone he'd like to meet.

"Of course, it was done after his death," the shop owner went on.

Liam felt let down – ridiculously, he knew. Of course the subject of this painting was dead. But he looked so alive!

"It's a beatification portrait," the man explained.

"You mean he was dead when it was done!" Liam said, rather stupidly. "I mean, he just seems so young – to be dead," he added lamely. "He was a saint?"

"Well. Certainly somebody thought so. Or hoped he would be. It was commissioned by a religious order during the cause for his beatification."

Liam understood. "A sort of advert. A bit of promotion." This portrait before him must be early twentieth century, he thought, but progressive for its time because the face of holiness for centuries had been lean, ascetic, distant and this portrait's candour and warmth would have been unusual. It was the sort that would be done today when approachability was to be emphasized for a more touchy-feely age: the saint as someone-you'd-like.

"It's late eighteenth century," the shop owner said.

"But he's so...." Liam was lost for words.

"Modern?"

"He's like someone you'd meet any day!"

"And he's very special." The shop owner pulled up a chair so that the two of them considered the painting together.

Liam felt obscurely privileged, then recognised that he was feeling the awe that comes from being in the presence of beauty. "Who is he?" he asked, aware of an excitement, like the anticipation on the point of meeting someone significant.

"Antonio Tramasco."

The name meant nothing. The shop owner shook his head regretfully. "He was well-known... at one time. The founder of...." He named a religious order familiar to Liam.

"But Alberetti founded them."

"Co-founded," the man corrected him. He sat back in his chair. "Tramasco was the real inspiration. It is to him they owe their charism but they chose to forget that."

"Why? Didn't he become a saint?"

"His process was halted. Very close to beatification. Some letters were found and the order withdrew of its own volition. It's a wonder this painting survived."

"How did you find it?"

"It's a little speciality of mine – these beatification portraits. Saints always sell. Archives clamour for them. I've been keeping an eye open – mildly, you know – for Tramasco, for a long time."

Liam watched him look at the portrait, not with avidity, not as an object of profit, but with a sad affection. He was the more surprised then when the man added, glancing at Liam, "People pay for things they love – and for things they fear." Liam, irritated at being out of his depth, moved to get up but the man laid a restraining hand on his arm. "Am I too cryptic? I guessed you wouldn't know." He smiled, waiting till Liam sat down again. "I am a businessman." Liam nodded impatiently. "I see you arrive... outside my window. I think at first – trouble! But then it seemed, perhaps not. I watched you. Very unguarded!" He laughed. "You were seeing nothing. But I saw you. Now, my young friend – because you *are* young (with all due respect for your station in life) – you were in the grip of some great emotion and Monsignor O'Reilly is in town." Liam was astonished. "Do you not wear the same habit? The esteemed O'Reilly is a customer of mine. He will buy this painting. He is a connoisseur." At Liam's scorn towards this assessment he leant forwards in amused chastisement, saying, "My friend! My friend! He collects items of archival interest. Tramasco's order flourishes, does it not, and in an area of work similar to yours?"

"Yes?"

"Almost – were it conceivable – competitors?"

Liam began to see. But even so! "He wouldn't buy it just so they couldn't have it. And I suppose they would want it. Even if he's a bit in the shade he's still their co-founder."

"Yet you've never heard of him. He is in darkness, not shade. Even though it was to him that God spoke and without him the order would not exist. They have hidden him well. Why should they put him on display now, whereas...." He looked at Liam. "Would our O'Reilly hide him?"

Liam considered. O'Reilly would enjoy the drama, taking the portrait out for a select few. If there was some scandal attached to it, even a mild one, it would provide an opportunity for barbed witticisms at the other order's expense. How distasteful!

He became aware of the shop owner's eyes on him. "I am a businessman. I saw you, and now you will tell O'Reilly about the portrait and I will contact Tramasco's order and tell *them*, and then business will be brisk!" He smiled. Liam was about to be indignant but the man pre-empted him. "Don't worry. I will sell to O'Reilly because otherwise this portrait will disappear for good. It will be safe with O'Reilly."

Liam was reluctant to relinquish his indignation even though he knew the man had read O'Reilly aright. The shop owner looked sad. "At least it will be safe," he repeated. He gazed at the portrait and Liam followed suit. They sat side by side for some time. Tramasco's handsome, reposeful face was impressive. It seemed to Liam that he looked happy; at once purposeful and fulfilled. "I probably am looking at his essence. An icon of goodness," he thought. At last Liam asked, "What did he do wrong?"

The shop owner sighed. "I think he was a man ahead of his time. He fell in love."

Not that! The most banal of falls, Liam thought bitterly, disappointed.

"Not in the way you think," said the shop owner. "He fell in love with a man." He scrutinised Liam, who felt himself flushing. "He wrote some letters... before he drowned. They didn't come to light for some time. When they did...."

"He was scuppered!" Liam knew he was being brutal, taking an unpleasant pleasure in Tramasco's downfall.

"His chances of sainthood were, yes, for the time, but times change."

"You can't have a saint with a gay lover!" Liam stood. He longed to get away.

"Who said he had a lover?" demanded the shop owner. "I said he fell in love with a man. There's nothing dishonourable in that."

Liam spluttered. "Dishonour comes, not from the feelings, but from what is done because of them." They were both standing now. "Look at this face," the shop owner demanded. "Do you see dishonour there? I have seen some of those letters and there's nothing in them that doesn't speak of devotion and sacrifice. I say 'love' and you hear something sordid. He *is* a saint! A saint for *our* age." Liam headed for the door. "My regards to Monsignor, remember."

Liam found the shop door locked. Calmly the owner walked to it, saying, "I intend to find out more about Antonio Tramasco and O'Reilly will help me do it – for the wrong reasons. But as you – a clever young man – know, O'Reilly is not as clever as he thinks." He held Liam's gaze challengingly, making him feel the implied rebuke, through the implied comparison, before he unlocked the door and released him into the street.

Liam chose to sit on a stone bench by the road along the Tiber because the roar of the traffic hurtling past cocooned him. He needed to think. He reflected on Tramasco's portrait, its hieratic pose of benediction. "They loved him," he thought, "those brothers of his who commissioned the portrait." Tramasco must have looked at them like that and they wanted to feel that look again. They didn't portray him as an ascetic, a penitent or a man of action but as a man in the act of bestowing blessing and – he had to admit it – transmitting love, the presence of love. He imagined meeting Tramasco. "What if he had fallen in love with *me*?"

He was flooded with sorrow, then with a dreadful sense of being crumpled in a heap. If he were to die now what would – could – be painted? A cocky sneer, an aggressive tilt of the head and a cynical expression; perhaps one hand thrust out to the side to keep others back out of his way? And if he died in thirty or forty years' time? He pictured O'Reilly's desiccated features.

He nearly cried aloud. Donal had been ashamed of him this morning because his love was not blind. "He has *seen* me!" Liam realised with alarm. He had been seen, right through to his clenched heart. And then? Liam made himself re-live the unfolding of his fingers, the touch of lips in his palm. He stood, abruptly. Donal loved him despite everything. How often had he himself preached that to people, telling them that that is how God loves them: "despite everything"?

Cautiously, he approached the concept of Donal's being in love with him. He could only see… Donal... being Donal. He could see himself. He let his memory range, but with this new information, and time and again, Donal's generosity and affection were obvious and his own careless acceptance of what he regarded as his due. Had he not paused to consider this dynamic? Yes. Now and then. He felt shame creep to every pore. He broke into a sweat. He had taken and taken. Was that not a form of collusion?

Collusion! In what? What had Donal done that was wrong? In fact... the wonder was how Donal had managed to love so much while being in love. Liam's own experiences of that had been characterised by possessiveness and appetite. Donal had curbed the desire for a response. "He loves me," Liam realised, "without asking anything in return." He was overwhelmed afresh.

He had to move. The traffic came back into earshot. The car. The keys were in his pocket so O'Reilly and Donal must be marooned!

Back at the Vatican he let O'Reilly's fury assail him without defending himself, standing with his head bowed. "Have you nothing to say for yourself?" the older man demanded eventually. "No ingenious explanation? No word of wisdom?"

Liam raised his eyes, but to Donal's face, and said, "I can't see what's in front of me, Monsignor. That's true."

"Well, I'm glad that's plain to you," snapped O'Reilly.

Liam continued to look at Donal, hoping to signal a willingness to reconnect. Donal, bravely, as Liam now realised, looked steadily, painfully, back. O'Reilly, feeling ignored, extended his tirade as he marched them towards the car.

Once they were seated, Liam turned to O'Reilly and said, "I have a message for you."

ACTING ABBY

There's something about an empty theatre – no matter how long you've been in the business, no matter how many wives or matriarchs or sluts you've played. I come in sometimes, in that hour or so when it's too early to be in the dressing room but there's not enough time to go anywhere. Besides, I don't always know where I am when we're on tour; don't know what's open or where anything is. Here, out front, it's almost home, no matter where the theatre is.

I sit and look. All these seats, expectant, focused on the stage. A pub interior, this one. Centre stage, a bar counter, backed by rows of gleaming bottles. In the middle of the shelves, an empty doorway, a narrow column of blackness. A curtain hangs over it: long beaded strings. A great touch that, I think – inspired – because the backstage draughts shiver the beads every now and then and, though everything around that curtain is static, an invisible finger glides across the curtain like a harpist's, releasing a ripple of movement. There's a perpetual suspense as to who – someone, surely – is about to emerge through that slit, through those hanging fringes and... tell us what it's all about.

That's why people come to the theatre. To be told something. Something worth knowing. They come. I hope! They come and I step forward from the dusty darkness behind the curtain and I tell them....

It's a good script. And the part gives me something to get my teeth into. Never met the author. A man. You can feel him trying to understand her – Abby. She's a bit of a bitch. That's what you think. Sharp little mind. Snip, snip, snip, she goes, at the husband. *Squirk! Squeak!* with the clean-clean linen cloth on the glasses. He hates that sound. Alan does the almost-wince really well. He grabs it back at the last moment. He wouldn't want to give her the satisfaction. *Squirk! Squirk!* she goes with the cloth. The audience get it. Alan and me work it up nicely till they're on the edge of their seats and wanting to yell, "Stuff that tea-towel down her gullet! Go on, mate!"

And then, when they see how the pieces fall into place, they're guilty, 'cos those glasses are all she's got. Screwing the tops on bottles just so, adjusting beer mats, everlastingly wiping the counter. He's gambled it all away and there's nothing left and now they want her to reach out and grab him by that stupid *mein host* waistcoat he wears and bang his head on the counter.

Though I don't think she's that type. She'd do something major. Flood the cellar or something. Beer everywhere. Is that possible? Beer kegs bumping into each other in the darkness – a mini Titanic! The delivery hatch flung open and a shaft of light floods down and his agonised face on the brink: "No-ooo...!!"

Actually, she'd take the car and.... Well. Where would she go? Isn't that always the problem? I can see why the author keeps it small-scale. Most people's lives are small-scale. That's what's so awful when the Bad Thing happens: the life just bursts apart 'cos it wasn't meant to contain this much pain.

Like in floods. Those pictures in the papers where someone's sitting, stunned, on a roof, with muddy water everywhere for miles. Someone's life has just burst apart and ejected him – out of his own life. Pop! Don't need you any more. Need more space. And from being the centre, he's on the edge – on the roof!

There was one bit on the news... I couldn't watch it all... where a teenager, some Asian teenager, all bony-limbed, was clinging for dear life to the branch of a tree and around him things were sweeping past. The water was pushing branches, a table, planks, fiercely along towards a rocky island. Things crashed and caught on it. A cat, four legs stiff, inside a basin, getting swirled along, and the water bashes the basin up against the rock and out springs the cat, dry as toast and you want to say to the boy – because we can see what he can't, that island – "Let go! Drop into the current. It'll take you."

And he doesn't and the water rises and he clings and clings... I didn't watch the end but you couldn't escape hearing about it – how he clung on till the water closed over his head and then, after a pause, you saw his body emerge – Pop! – swung out into the current and reaching the island after all. But he didn't leap up like the cat, being dead.

"What would you save?" They ask you that, don't they, in interviews. If there was a fire or a flood, like. People save such stupid things and they must be lying. Why would they tell the truth to a shiny mag? So that people like me can gloop it down and burp! They do lie. They must do. I would. I do.

No. I don't. Actually, I don't. I say, when people ask me gingerly about how I'm coping, "Well, my stuff is in people's houses, or garages, or sheds, or whatever! I just don't think about it too much when I'm touring." But I do. Except I turn away from it because it's pointless. I'll deal with it when the run's finished.

The flood came. My flood. It was a relief, in the end. Though I can't say it was a natural disaster, an act of God. I pulled out a few bungs, a few stoppers, myself. Yes, I did. Out they came. Pop! Pop! Pop! Down we went, husband, children, pets, house and car. I floated up and away, onto the wide, muddy water.

Poor Abby. The writer doesn't let her flood the cellar. He keeps her in the spotlight – writers are like that – a dry woman, squeaky-clean. "The baby," she says. We know about the blood, the dash to the hospital, the husband's promises – not so much as a doggie or even a scratch card ever again. He'd have promised anything in the panic! "The baby.... Sorry. I'm so sorry..." she says and he answers with a rustle of pages turning. The dry "flak" of newsprint shaken like a whip. Silence. The audience does the howling – in silence; in the silence where they watch her do nothing and then she lifts her hand... and picks up that tea-towel and *Squirk! Squeak! Squeak!* What else can she do?

They want to storm the stage and rip it to shreds, tear their clothes in a frenzy, mourn and wail. Anything but this stepping into the tomb of silence. *You'll die!* they want to shout. *Don't do it! It's behind you! The great black emptiness. Behind the beaded curtain. It's waiting for you! Say no! Get out of there!*

But she doesn't and they're exhausted by the end. Worn out with pity and vowing not to... not to... whatever it is she did. Do they look at her choice, I wonder; really turn the spotlight on themselves as they go home; as they lie in bed later on?

Because the audience knows he'd had the snip without telling her. All that time letting her believe the not getting pregnant was her fault, pretending to be sympathetic every month. Bastard.

I'd have done it myself, if I was her, even if it had to be with a smarmy bloke from the brewery. She does it for her husband. He *deserves* a baby. That seems obvious to her. And she thinks she's sparing his male pride. He'll never know, will he? Just a question of steering clear of DNA tests! A risk worth taking anyway. Not like he'd hand a baby back!

So down in the cellar she falls, in more ways than one, stumbling about in the nearly dark with the muscle-bound delivery man. Just in case. Just in case it's him, *mein host,* who's the problem and not her.

Who's shafted who? When she tells him, coyly thrilled like you're supposed to be, he doesn't look at all pleased. He looks totally bloody shocked!

The interval's then. *Who'll do what? Who'll we side with? Would you go that far? Stupid cow. He's a prick an' a half. But lots of blokes don't want kids − he's just doing something about it. Using his initiative.*

So the second half works every time because they don't know who to back – yet. She always gets them in the end. When they see her realize that he's sent the business down the Swanee and she still tries to keep afloat. And even after the miscarriage she grieves for his grief at their lost child. But the audience has seen him downing a private whiskey in relief.

Well, they despise him. All she says is, "My little piece of happiness." Those few months when she thought she'd made an island in the storm – when she *was* the island, sheltering its one little inhabitant. She bought baby clothes stoically – well, that's not in the script but I'm sure she would have. She'd have met other mothers in the store. "He's not with you, then?" Too busy, she'd say. But he's excited. Of course. Yes. Every time she asks him he says he is. Till she stops asking.

"My little piece of happiness". She says that and the audience understands. That fragile thing shining over the floods like a tiny star, over the waste of waters. Tiny light. Don't take that away. Leave me that at least. I'll die without it. Don't shut the trap door on me. Don't leave me here in the dark!

That's what I couldn't survive. I couldn't survive letting that go – letting my Dave go. If I let Dave go, I'll have nothing. No, I'll have plenty. Really. I'll have the kids – when I get to see them. But my little piece of happiness, that I cling to in the storm, Dave's voice that warms to me along the phoneline...! After the show, back in whatever digs, there's that to look forward to: his voice from a distance. And his shabbinesses don't matter and his dubious motives and his wife swearing theirs is an open marriage: stoically; and my husband, bitter and raging.

I can't let Dave go. If I let go, I'll sink. He tells me, "Don't let go. You're safe with me." Safe enough next year, and the next, and forever? "Don't let go!" And I don't. My little piece of happiness. It isn't enough. I know it isn't. Not for a whole lifetime. I cling to it – and you can understand?

IMPRESARIO

Beppe's father was small but very, very strong. His grip on Beppe's collar would not lessen till they reached the top of the stairs. Beppe could barely breathe but he writhed and kicked fiercely. Mamma's grip on his ankles made matters much, much worse. She wailed and pleaded, "No, Gino! He's a good boy! He meant to do it. He will do it!" as she tugged at his legs. They would strangle him between them! His father dragged harder, bumping Beppe's buttocks up each step and shouting, "A rope. A rope!" Bettina kicked Beppe nastily as she pushed upstairs waving a length of plastic clothesline. "Here, Papa!" she shrieked but Papa couldn't take it because, with Beppe in one hand, he was holding the accordion in the other.

Papa kicked the door open and shoved Beppe into the room, swinging him round so that he slid across the lino and hit the wall beneath the window. Papa brandished the accordion. "Stand up!" he yelled. "Stand up!" As Beppe reluctantly got to his feet his father was upon him, thrusting the accordion against his chest. Beppe instinctively gripped it – what a bloody weight! – and instantly his father was behind him, hoiking the straps over Beppe's shoulders and – what! – tying the accordion to his body with the clothesline. Beppe's mother knelt – to beg for mercy, he thought. About time. But no! She was turning on the miserable little gas fire in the hearth. "It's freezing, Gino," she muttered apologetically. Talk about accepting the situation. No more help from her, then. Beppe's father pushed her from the room. "Don't lie to me!" he bellowed at his son. "You say you practise, then do it!" He left. The key turned in the lock.

Beppe rushed to the door and shook the handle violently. The bulk of the accordion meant he could hardly reach to do it. It was nineteen-seventy-two. *No Body Played the Accordion.* It made no difference to bang on the wooden panels and shout and he would not resort to the heartfelt pleading that sometimes worked on his mother. He was a man. He would not plead. He would suffer! And plot his revenge.

First thing was to get this bloody thing off his chest. He felt around his back for the knot then paused to consider the consequences. He stopped. Papa was small and very, very strong. He himself was tall and.... He felt himself blush. It wasn't that he was untried. He was a good fighter but... against Papa? A man could not fight his own father.

It just wasn't fair. These old people, they held all the cards. At his age, Papa had had had the Second World War ahead of him. He had been with the anti-Fascist partisans. The very fact that he could seldom be persuaded to speak of it, just made it all the more impressive. It was mainly through Papa's friends that Beppe knew of these exploits. He was good at listening outside the door when they talked of themselves – the months starving in the mountains; the confusion as their allies abandoned and betrayed them; the shame of the terrible *resa dei conti*, the settling of accounts with unsupportive relatives and neighbours. It sounded as though they were discussing other people. They gave little sighs, of wonderment and regret. Then they'd start singing in their harsh-voiced harmonies: songs of the peaks and pastures, of sweet girls with long plaits of brown hair... and the accordion would be called for and he'd have to disappear as Papa emerged from the room to fetch it. Papa would play. Shouldn't he give up at his age? He was fifty-something!

"And I'm fifteen!" Beppe thought with acute horror. The accordion weighed him down. The old people – they would make him carry their homesickness, their exile and nostalgia. He *was* home. Cardiff was his home. He went to the window. The street outside was quiet and dark. Eight o'clock. Raining. Prison. Some home! He felt very sorry for himself. Nobody played the accordion. Especially not someone like Beppe Salvemini. Beppe. Beppe! He didn't want to be a Beppe. Sounded like some stupid little puppet you could knock down time and again. Beppe. Giuseppe. Joseph. Joe. Joe Salvemini. That was a *bit* better. At least it sounded more like a boxer or a gangster or a – yeah! – criminal mastermind. He played some ominous chords. *Dio*! He hadn't meant to do that. It was giving in.

It was very, very cold. He went to the gas fire and turned his back to it. Maybe the plastic cord would burn through – not before it burnt through him, he realised, deflated. He felt the fierce heat warm his back and thighs and stretched his hands backwards to the fire. Cardiff was bloody cold. The old guys were right about that. Not like their sunny homeland. Beppe smiled, remembering holidays there, when it was so hot he'd been glad to snooze through the afternoons and be up late, late, late in the soft darkness.

Rain flung itself against the windowpane like an insult, like mockery. If his friends could see him now! Living with a tyrant, that's what it was. Work, work, work. Study, study. What for? There was money to be made and not the hard way, like the old man, laying stone floors, coming home white with dust, complaining of aching knees and customers who didn't appreciate 'the real thing'; going on about how terrazzo depended on a good foundation and all the painstaking rolling, grinding, polishing; and about the mosaic floor-work he used to do in Italy. But still, Papa wouldn't go back there, would he? Oh, no. Not enough work there. But he didn't like it here either. "Those priests, they should beat you! Too soft!" he'd yell. "What sort of a Catholic school is that?"

Beppe had begged to be allowed to work in a restaurant. He would look good, very good, swivelling between tables, though he never said that to Papa. Somewhere classy. But Papa refused to let him anywhere near 'that business'. Lots of their friends were in it. What was he so afraid of? Or so sad about? The way he had looked at Beppe once, reaching out to touch his face, shaking his head as though he'd lost something. Beppe knew there was nothing wrong with his face. It was a great face. The best Beppe could get out of him was a quiet, "My son. My son." and some stuff about respect and being your own boss and getting a trade. On your knees all day? No, thanks! With a bit of experience, he could get work anywhere. London was only a train ride away. Beppe could hear the trains now as they headed east, out of Wales.

Beppe went to the window. Down below, the gutters were flowing noisily. Rain filled the street. He wandered back to the hearth, wretched. He would die here, cold and miserable, and be forgotten. He found himself playing the melancholy chorus of one of those mountain songs. Just right! Let the old man hear him. He'd be sorry when it was too late. He played a little more, then tune after tune, from memory. He could hold a sobbing top section till his heart was fit to break then bring it glissando-ing down, giving it plenty of elbow for effect and swinging down and up from the hips, making the fringe around the bottom of the instrument jiggle.

He was in exile too! Cut off from life and youth. He could be out there right now: smiling at the customers, being extra nice to his favourites, seeing a bit of life, in the bright lights, pocketing money, having fun! But where was he? His father's prisoner, because Papa called it lying – saying you'd practised when you hadn't – and getting his mother to 'lie' too. Of course he did. He needed back-up, didn't he? Papa called this the worst of all. Well, he meant to do much, much worse!

Beppe pulled some sheet music off the music stand, sat down on a chair close to the fire and balanced the papers on his knee. This was a fancy piece, a show-off. He couldn't see the music properly but it was so cold that he didn't want to leave the heat. He propped the sheets on the top of the gas-fire frame. A trill and an arpeggio. Like that! And again. The big old sash window shook in a blast of wind that startled Beppe with its violence. He looked over his shoulder, expecting to see someone glaring in. But he was on the first floor. He smiled at himself and turned back and suddenly there were flames before his eyes. He leapt away but they didn't stop! The music was on fire – and the fringes! He beat at them but the fabric of the accordion had caught, and the sleeve of his jumper. He yelled. There were flames at his feet among discarded music, and stuff on the mantelpiece was going up too.

"Fire! I'm on fire! Papa!" He rushed to the door. His jumper was burning across his back. His hair! His face! He couldn't get free of this burning thing on his chest. Why didn't they come? They didn't believe him. They wouldn't come. He would die! He stumbled to the window. Rain! He drew back and then launched himself through the glass.

Beppe's father rushed out into the drenching night when he saw a strange flaming thing swoop past the downstairs window. He flung himself to his knees beside his son who lay humped over, a smouldering heap. He kept saying, "Not a liar, Beppe. Just not a liar. That's all." The neighbours had to pull him off. Beppe's mother talked to the ambulancemen. She was very, very calm.

Forty years later, Joe Salvemini was sitting in a welter of noise and glitz, at a big, circular table right under the Awards podium in Cardiff's premier venue. He couldn't have heard himself speak, if he'd tried. Shards of projected light crashed through the darkness over dozens of tables, some square, some round, arranged like pieces in a pattern. Not quite a mosaic, he thought. More like terrazzo. He could see bits of people: an arm, a flank, a lifted hand, and so many open mouths.

Seated around his table were his young men, handsome in their dinner jackets, all black-haired, their teeth glittering as they bent towards one another. He was the gem in the ring. They were mostly imports, hungry but undisciplined. It was a craft, entertainment. Nightclubs, casinos, personal services – those especially – didn't run themselves. A careful arrangement of relationships and obligations had to be kept in place. Ingenuity, deftness, flair and more than one kind of flexibility were needed but who around this table was steadily assessing, selecting, readying himself for an introduction?

Joe was indignant and resentful. He wouldn't carry them forever. They were here to work! Yet every year's cohort protested at the ban on girlfriends. "I don't bring my wife," he would say. "This is business!" A sorry business this, the highlight of the media year. He looked around the cavernous space. As chic as an aircraft-hangar and as empty. The Welsh couldn't do glamour. It ended up crass, after all he'd done for them. He had kept his Franco out of all this: eighteen and headed for university. And Josephine. Sweet sixteen. She was fetched and watched. It was his duty, as a father. They would not get their teeth into *her*.

He was tired. Here he could sit undisturbed, wrapped in noise. He felt old. His body was heavy that had been so lithe, so admired. He had got what he wanted. He knew what he did, what he sold.

"Papa," he heard himself explain, "I am an artist." His father was kneeling, preparing the surface of a floor, bent to the ground. "I am an artist, Papa." The old man seemed to hear and yet to turn away. "Papa," he insisted, fanning his colourful achievements out on the dust, pushing away tools and chippings so his father could see their variety and scale, their cost and ambition. A glance. No more. "Papa, look!" Joe was begging now. He twisted low to see up into that lined face. Did he have to spell it out? "Escape, papa. I sell escape." The trowel kept sweeping, left to right and back, with its familiar rasp and sigh. Joe was suddenly flooded with grief and rage. "You should have stood up to me. You gave in! From guilt. What's a scorched neck and burnt hands?"

He lurched up from the table and pushed through the chairs, the bodies. Where was the exit? Someone attempted to hug him. He pushed her off. He waded through the bright lights of the foyer and out down the steps. Cameras flashed. He veered away towards a taxi.

As the streets sped past, the driver kept asking, "Where to?"

At last Joe Salvemini answered, "I don't know."

That, at least, he thought, is the truth.

THE TRIUMPH

In the consulting room she sat with her legs dangling over the edge of the examination couch. Good legs for forty-two, she thought, as a handsome young doctor considered them with an air of scrupulous concern. His white coat accentuated the darkness of his skin. Middle Eastern, she supposed. Persian, he told her when she asked. She was struck by that, since she thought people said Iranian these days. 'Persian' suited his cultured air. He was both deferential and aristocratic, a charming combination. He asked questions delicately, waiting humbly for her answers, though the fact that he was kneeling in front of her no doubt enhanced that impression.

The varicose veins, he said, were not pronounced. Treatment was a possibility but not urgent. How much pain? he asked. Lots, she emphasized, determining not to be too ready to oblige the waiting list by downplaying her symptoms. "It's pretty bad now," she said. "Won't it be worse if they're not dealt with?" He looked at her doubtfully. "Given my medical history," she pleaded, "to have this on top of everything else!" He had read her notes, surely.

"It is borderline. I must ask Mr. Fielding. I could not recommend you for treatment without checking with him." He lifted one hand, turning it palm upward as though proffering it for fate to drop something beneficial into it. How graceful he was! He made to stand but suddenly he cried out in agony and clutched the couch, stuck in a crouched position, his head almost in her lap, unable to move further. "Doctor!" she cried, in alarm.

He gasped. "Nothing! Nothing."

She slid off the couch and pushed a chair towards him. He collapsed into it. His beautiful eyes were blank with pain. He closed them. His forehead was damp, his knuckles white. He let go of the couch. Recovering a little, he straightened very slowly. She handed him a plastic beaker of water from the little sink. He looked, she thought, dreadfully tired all of a sudden. She sighed. She knew how pain can hollow you out and now, she could tell, he was disheartened and embarrassed, or even ashamed.

Their eyes met. "Is it your back?" she asked.

He nodded. "It happens. I don't know why."

"But you will. Someone's looking, aren't they?" What was she doing? He could have cancer or AIDS or heart failure. She shouldn't stumble about offering platitudes, and he was the doctor not she, but when he raised his eyes sadly she wanted to help. "It's tough," she said. "You're doing well." He smiled, just slightly, whether in contradiction or rueful agreement she couldn't tell.

Suddenly there was less space in the room as the door, opening sharply inwards, missed her by inches and a blue suit entered. In it was a short man of about forty, speaking to someone in the outer office even as he came in. "Two! Not ten past! Tell him I said that!" He started when he saw them, unexpectedly close: the doctor in the chair, the patient, bare-legged, where she should not be. He saw the beaker of water and their self-conscious expressions. She saw contempt on his face as he watched the Persian struggle to stand; slim, tall and hurting.

"Let's have the patient where we can see her, shall we, Dr. Houshmand?" The consultant, tucking a cardboard file of notes under his arm like a swagger-stick, cocked his head to one side, insolently, she thought. He showed no sympathy for his colleague.

He asked for an assessment which Dr. Houshmand supplied respectfully. It was met with something very like a snort. Turning to her he sneered, "And you want surgery?"

"I want what's appropriate," she replied. She added, as pleasantly as she could manage, "You *are* Mr. Fielding, I suppose? Only you didn't happen to say when you came in."

He didn't deign to answer this. He put the file down and leafed through it, asking a few questions about medication, ending with, "No medication of any kind at all?" in a tone that conveyed that he thought she was a crank.

"No," she insisted. Really, he was not a pleasant man and seeing him next to handsome and courteous Dr. Houshmand did him no favours. His physique, his features, were mediocre. They seemed inadequate to contain his sizeable self-regard.

Had he read that thought? His lips tightened. He waved Dr. Houshmand brusquely out of his way and stood in front of her. He seemed to be waiting for something – the chair that Dr Houshmand placed for him. Carefully hitching up the knees of his trousers, Mr. Fielding seated himself regally in front of her legs.

It was indeed a beautiful suit, she acknowledged silently as he lifted one of her heels, then the other, and poked his forefinger along her shins. An unusually blue blue for a British man. It would stand out in a crowd. It said status, success. A considered choice.

He pursed his lips, continuing to press and probe. "A little vain?" he said lightly.

"Where?" she asked, then his smirk revealed her gullibility.

"Old age comes to us all, you know," he said. "Sometimes we find that ladies want our help for cosmetic reasons. Turn around, please."

"I brought my legs along to be looked at. That's all I can do," she said coldly. "This leg hurts. You'll have an opinion."

"Oh, I do. A little *vein*, just here." She stayed silent. He pressed her calves between finger and thumb along their length. "Well." He threw his voice in Houshmand's direction. "Shall we allow vanity to prevail?"

"No, Mr. Fielding!" Dr. Houshmand was shocked. "A little vein is no basis for...."

"A play on words!" Fielding snapped irritably, as though lumbered with a stooge who couldn't play along. Houshmand looked confused. "I think we can consider Mrs. Matthews's legs as candidates for treatment," said Fielding. "Not stripping, though. Injection. Stripping would be...." He scrutinised her legs, head on one side.

"In vain," she said, very seriously.

He looked up sharply but she met his gaze deadpan.

"Contra-indicated," he snapped pompously.

"A play on words," she smiled.

"Not one I haven't heard before," he sneered.

"Such an elegant double negative."

He avenged himself. "It will hurt," he warned, with relish, "but that's life. We must grin and bear it – some of us better than others." He looked, as he sprang briskly to his feet, at Dr. Houshmand. He settled his cuffs so that their glittering cuff-links displayed themselves. He glanced at his shoes and she saw they were immaculate. He was a well-armoured man. His supremacy was incontrovertible. He could now afford to condescend. "I'll take you round to Dr. Preece myself – he does the injecting – as he may well wonder why he's being asked to fit such a borderline case into his busy schedule."

He swept from the room; swept as though trailing voluminous draperies or enveloped in the billows of an academic gown, its sleeves swelling in the breeze of his momentum. Staff in the outer office paused as he entered (deferentially she assumed) and she and Dr. Houshmand followed in his wake and then she saw it!

Across the back of the blue suit was a huge, white splatter of bird shit. Involuntarily she glanced at Dr. Houshmand, startled. He looked at her in alarm. Other faces in the office, who must have seen Mr. Fielding on his way in, were, she realised, concealing amusement. She saw that Mr. Fielding was reading the charged atmosphere as a fitting tribute to his prowess, because he smiled complacently and lifted his head. "We are the vanquished he is leading in chains," she thought. "This is his triumphal march.". She swung a glance at her fellow captive. For a moment he nobly resisted looking at her but then he smiled, a marvellous smile which he quickly folded away and they continued with downcast eyes to process out of the office suite into a public corridor where Mr. Fielding's persona, like a prow, cleared a passage through the flood of hospital-users that swept towards them. Abruptly he turned left, pushed open a door and disappeared inside. Without looking at Dr. Houshmand she said quietly to him, "I hope your back gets better."

Mr. Fielding re-appeared on the threshold. "You should find it all satisfactory," he said. Carefully keeping any compassion out of her expression (because he would interpret that in retrospect as pity) she thanked him. He headed for his department. She paused just long enough to look at Dr. Houshmand. He nodded, a little sadly. Yes, he would be magnanimous. He followed his superior back through the crowd.

WITNESS

Harman had turned for a moment, as he waited for the front door to be opened, feeling himself scrutinised beneath the imperious arc of the security light. Despite his terrible anxiety, he had wondered at the way it cast itself into the yard and struck the dank Fermanagh acres beyond its reach into a solid, black block. Now, inside the house, he felt himself somehow accused. Pastor McKittrick was.... He was.... He seemed to be choking on the news that Harman had just brought him and he swung away, his physical vehemence clearly conveying, *To hear it from **you**!*

"Muriel!" he roared.

The phone rang as Muriel McKittrick put her head around the door, already looking at Harman for clues − he'd rushed by her into the house with a mere, breathless, "The pastor?" "Tell her!" McKittrick ordered Harman, without taking his eyes from his wife.

"There's been... an incident," Harman began. "At the Gospel Hall. Jack Clemans and Margaret Baird maybe. Shooting.... A shooting. People wounded. I came to tell...." He glanced at McKittrick. Surely it was a husband's place to break such news to his wife? But McKittrick continued to glare at Muriel and so Harman stumbled on. "We were just ending the service, singing the last hymn...."

"Are You Washed In The Blood Of The Lamb?", McKittrick cried. "Do you hear that, Muriel?" She put a hand over her mouth. "Do you hear that?" McKittrick persisted. "Go on!" he commanded Harman, who protested, "Pastor!"

Husband and wife were fixed on each other and silent, so he continued. "The gunmen came into the porch, firing, and that's where Jack was hit, and he... he fell into the hall and staggered up the aisle with them behind him, firing away. And Jack kept coming...." Harman stopped. The poor woman knew enough now. The phone rang on.

"And they....?" McKittrick prompted him but he shook his head so it was McKittrick who went on, "And they got him by the shoulders and turned him around, and they looked him in the eye and shot him in the chest."

Harman wondered at the pastor's determination to spare his wife nothing. It was cruel – and would they not answer that phone!

Muriel McKittrick was white-faced but now she held on to the door-edge with both hands and her lips were compressed into a tight line. "Mr. Harman," she said suddenly, "this is dreadful for you." Turning to her husband she asked, "What will you do?"

He looked at her with such contempt that Harman thought he was about to spit on her but he just pushed past her out of the room. She leant her head onto her hands where they held the door. "God," he heard her say, tonelessly.

Should he stay and comfort her? Not when so many... so many people.... The phone, that had stopped briefly, rang again. He picked it up. "No. It's Eric Harman here. I've told the pastor. He's.... I don't know.... He's left the house." He heard a car start up. "What? Yes. I'll tell him."

She hadn't moved. Harman was perplexed and then suddenly exhausted. He sat down abruptly, his hands hanging between his knees. He shook his head. What was wrong with his ears? They felt full of something. The phone rang again. Just as if it were his own home, he leapt up with an exclamation and picked up the receiver. He stuffed it under a cushion and sat down again and only then did the action seem out of place. He had to clear his head. He was trembling. He looked up. No drink in this house.

"If you look under the kitchen sink," he heard her whisper, still not moving, "you'll find a dram."

Gingerly, in the kitchen, he opened cupboards. He sniffed at an unlabelled bottle. He found a glass, then took a second one. She let go of the door when he returned. They drank. She spluttered but downed the measure doggedly. Then, at last, she left the doorway. "Tell me," she said.

He told her, half-hearing his own horror and, bizarrely, he sensed, his excitement. For what had he seen? Jack Clemans's comic turn, dragging one leg and grunting. Margaret Baird up at the front, turning with lips pursed, ready to castigate, her fat cheeks puckered in practised disapproval, and then her doubling over but jerking up and back sharply as though someone had goosed her and she had seemed to recline languidly, still holding her hymn book open. And then a man – a stranger – in the aisle had turned his way. The roaring! The red plastic seats suddenly higher than his head. The metal chair legs – stems and trunks and undergrowth! He had crawled, desperately, cravenly…!

He felt a pressure on his hand. She was offering more whiskey. He shook his head. "I don't know how many died," he said. "It was still going on when I got out and I'd been late so my car was, y'know, first out and I just thought, 'Tell the pastor!' Was that... stupid?" He looked up at her.

She shook her head.

"No. Stupid," he insisted and then contradicted himself. "Och, I don't know."

"Norman McAllister?" she asked

"He was leading the singing, of course. I don't know."

She sighed.

"He's a good young man," Harman assured her, pointlessly now, perhaps, he thought.

She nodded.

"Very keen, Norman," he added, helplessly. She folded her lips, one into the other, till they disappeared. He stared at her. She had not gone plump and comfortable like wives in their sixties do. He had always admired her. "I should be doing something," he said.

"Like what?" She looked hard at him. "Stanley shouldn't have made you do that." He pretended not to know what she meant. "Making you repeat it all to me. He was punishing you." She paused. "Did they enjoy it?"

He was puzzled.

"Those men, those gunmen."

He considered. "They... they were... workman-like."

She seemed satisfied. Why was that the right answer, he wondered. She obliged. "If you're going to kill someone, I think it's better − not so evil − if you don't enjoy it." She considered and added, "Though I imagine the actual doing of it is satisfying in a way."

He said something he was sure of, "Pastor McKittrick was very angry."

"He missed his chance."

"His...?"

"I told him to stay at home."

"Thank God...!" Harman began but she went on without pause, "Yes, 'Stay at home', I said. 'You're jealous, Stanley. You're afraid that young Norman McAllister is a better preacher than you and you stand in his way. Is it God's work you're doing or your own?' He was furious... inside, I mean. Not outside. No. He stayed home."

The doorbell rang and she went to it. Harman heard an exchange between an agitated male voice and her near silence. When she returned, alone, she said, "Norman's dead. Well, now. I did God's work, all right!" She laughed.

He stood up, appalled. "Mrs. McKittrick...!"

"I've been married nearly forty-one years. I can tell you exactly what my husband will say. It'll be, 'Norman the martyr. Dying with his flock'. Poor Stanley."

He could think of no response. She picked up the bottle and secured its cap. She glanced around for the phone. He fetched it from under the cushion. She replaced it, saying, "It won't be easy for you." She saw that he hadn't understood her. "She's a good wife to him."

How she had leapt ahead, he realised! His own son. His Catholic daughter-in-law.

"And you're good to *her*," she insisted. "I see you driving her and your grandchildren to Mass. Oh, Eric!" she cried. "Don't be ashamed!"

"I have to go," he announced stiffly.

"Don't... *leave* us. Some will think you should, after this."

"I have to go," he repeated.

Next evening, Harman saw Pastor McKittrick on the TV news, "I say, as a shepherd of God's people, to the God-appointed powers of this land, take up the sword to destroy evil in our midst. Those men who cut down the flower of our flock will not be forgiven by me nor by any Christian man nor by God himself till they repent their sin. No forgiveness without repentance." Then he added, with relish, Harman thought, "And to those who would take the part of the men of blood I say, 'Come ye out from among them'."

"You were not at the service?" the reporter asked.

"No," McKittrick replied curtly. "But..." he went on, with a fierce energy that obliged the reporter to stay with him, "a tape-recording was being made of that service and this very day, three young men accepted Christ into their lives just through hearing it. The blood of the martyrs is a powerful witness."

Harman thought of his son. Sam would never repent of his marriage to Eilish. Nor *should* he − the conviction shot through Harman. He groaned.

Harman went out into the yard and looked across his fields. The trees dripped with recent rain. Everything had been rinsed and the clouds were bundling themselves away over the hills. "No," he told God. "I'm too old."

But God persisted.

"Not me, Lord. Not me. I crawled away." But he couldn't make himself believe that had been wrong.

He had no excuse. He was to be a witness.

INTIMACY

She was speaking. She felt how earnestly she was trying to tell him exactly how it had been.

"I'm packing a suitcase. I'm focused but anxious – working against the clock – and against space, because things get to places. They get under this and stuffed inside that and when you find them you have to decide whether you really need them or not – weighing things in the balance: Yes? No?

"I'm in an airport space. It's walled by windows. People criss-cross on their way here and there and all the time there's this pervasive worry, the background to everything, the atmosphere. I concentrate on the suitcase. It's half-full. Suddenly everything snaps – in two – and dread floods me so I'm instantly weightless. The baby! Where…? Where is he? A sturdy, beautiful boy, not walking yet but mobile. I look around. No. And again, no. Not here nor anywhere I can see. But he was right here! He was my responsibility. I dash from one person to another, a madwoman, incoherent. People go carefully blank. They don't get it. Is it to do with them?

"I must choose. Do I look for an official or use time to check the nearest exit? I run – bang open a door – and I'm staring down a flight of metal steps and the sea's prowling and spitting up from these black rocks below. Too late!

"I wake. Again. For years I've had this dream. I've lost the baby. It's always me in charge of a baby and something goes wrong, something is jeopardized and it's my fault. I wake at that stage. I wasn't where I should have been. I didn't do what I should have done. I was responsible and I failed." Her eyes were fixed on the plate-glass window of the café but her gaze was on the inner scene. "It's always somebody else's baby," she added, wonderingly.

A tiny movement underneath her hand made her blink. The tablecloth was moving, somehow. His face replaced the vision that had occupied her. Like a blow to the head. She recoiled from the sight of him. He had turned pale. The forefinger of his right hand was pressed to the neck of a teaspoon on the table. His finger-tip had gone white with the force. The teaspoon edged forward under the pressure, the tablecloth gathering up into a long, looming breaker. A burst of power would send the coffee cups and the flimsy café table flying through the window – with a roar!

She was shocked. She had gone too far. This revelation to someone like him! She knew she was still in awe of him. His remarkable good looks attracted constant attention so he was circumspect always. He had certainly encouraged her to talk whenever business had thrown them together. He had seemed to get a mild enjoyment from her ricocheting subject choices though he never tried to follow her darting course. A nod, pursed lips, a shrug, a shift of his weight – even a smile, those were his responses, and perhaps another question. Yet she trusted him. She sometimes felt she was like a timid but promising protégée watched by the maestro and that one day he would lift a finger and say, "Yes, but *this*.... " And a world would open up. Until now!

He stood. She said hurriedly, "I'm sorry. What a bore I am. You hardly know me." She took her bag and pushed back her chair. "Other people's dreams... not fascinating, are they? I suppose I think that if I tell them – the dreams – I'll see what they mean and then I'll be able to do something; they'll be useful somehow, you know, give me a handle...." As she manoeuvred through the café furniture he tossed some money to a waitress. He held the door for her and she felt herself scuttle out, the guilty party.

On the pavement she was acutely aware of the big café windows, like lenses, magnifying her predicament. Why did he stop right here in full view of everyone? What he said surprised her, "We need somewhere we can talk." He indicated she should go with him. She saw a woman in the café coolly withdraw her gaze and raise an eyebrow to her friend who stared with open curiosity out through the glass at such an ill-matched pair: handsome and plain; suave and dowdy.

Half an hour later they were in the City Cemetery, a jumbled repository for the dead. Idiosyncratic Victorian monuments asserted themselves alongside the commonplace: 'Look at me. I'm dead – but still worth looking at. Look!' During the drive he hadn't spoken, nor had she. He hadn't said where they were going. Part of her was amazed that she was putting herself in his hands like this but she had a penalty to pay, didn't she?

They stood by a grave in a neglected area, in a dip in the cemetery which was hidden from the rest of the extensive site. They stood by a single plot. The gravestone had no lettering at all. He bent down to its base and parted the coarse grasses. She saw something small, carved there close to the earth: a Madonna lily with one bud. He did not look at her but she knew he wanted confirmation. "A lily," she said. He straightened up. There was a message here, a statement. She desperately didn't want to fail him. The message must follow on from what she'd said in the café. "A baby?" she ventured.

"And the mother."

Her mind sped across possibilities. His baby? Someone else's baby? His wife… lover… victim?

"They died because of me," he said. She saw him in her own anonymous, vast space of transients and provisional encounters where a baby is a speck of dust, here, then gone, and − in the same moment − with the ground gritty and solid beneath her feet, she saw him by this scruffy patch which was quilted with weeds and knot-grass, seeded with flesh. "I wasn't where I should have been," he told the stone.

Her nightmare.

They drove to her house in silence, apart from a few directions she gave him. As she closed her front door behind him and heard his car drive off, she had to gather her energy together in order to move along the hallway and up the stairs to her flat. In the kitchen she switched on the kettle. She lifted the lid of the blue pottery jar of tea bags. The kettle purred on to its climax as she stood looking into the jar, her fingers holding the lid by its delicate little pinnacle. She replaced the lid. It settled onto the inner rim with a tiny, satisfied clink. In place. Right.

She put both hands around the jar. What was inside, glimpsed, had to stay un-probed, sacrosanct. What he had given her had to be enough. How did that feel? Right.

Terrible. To be at once singled out and shut out. Bowing to this, she bowed over the jar. Terrible. Enough.

Instantly a tiny barb of joy lodged in her heart, burying itself deep, like a seed finding its place.

How much he had given her!

And he was right to believe she deserved it.

REPAIR

I'm called in after a death – not immediately but when the funeral's over and the task of sorting out the house and belongings has to be faced. People up and down this valley know I'm a bloke who's interested. Local, see. They know where I live, so I won't be off with the family silver. Not that there's much of that about. It's not what people here ever put their money into. Way more than a century ago, back when Coal was King in Wales, as they say, families in the boom times might splash out on a nice walnut bureau or a cabinet to show off the best china and these pieces hang on, here and there, among the old folk.

Sometimes I spot something the family hasn't valued much and I can tell them it's worth a bit. They appreciate that – most of them. I'm good at small repairs too. I get asked to see what I can do to mend this or that. I charge hardly anything but when I do see something I fancy I make a fair offer and mostly people are glad to be spared the hassle of putting it on the market. I've been at this now since long before I retired. Always been interested in old things, old houses. How do you know where you are unless you know where you've come from? Right?

Nine times out of ten these houses have seen a series of deaths and, like as not, those of a married couple. There's a kind of sameness about these houses, the houses of the dead – that's how I think of them. Ownership not yet transferred, if you like. Pending. There are lots of these houses. And I've got so I can read them.

This house, now, this particular house in Briwnant Street

(eighteen-eighties terraced, back extension nineteen-sixty − a DIY-job, corrugated PVC roof and all) the husband here was buried last week. This little house has an airless feel to it. Everything in it's ownerless, like. You'll get what I mean. The quilt on the bed in the big front room above? Nylon, thin, like something that's had the air let out − its cheap fibre filling showing through in patches − and it's flounced in an orangey pink that is, frankly, unlikely. His late wife, I bet, chose it when it seemed cheery and modern. She died ages ago so it looks, well, just too feminine − grotesque, even − given that everything else is... well, you can tell there's only been a man living here. The sheets beneath the quilt − lemon. A queasy mix. Life in this house shrank to one crucial room downstairs and now it has evaporated. Nothing of value here. So-so furniture. Everything used up to the point of exhaustion: painfully flattened toothpaste tube; lidless jar of half-burned candles. The people who lived here said to one another, 'Mustn't grumble' and they didn't. They 'got by'. For the sake of what? Myself, I get a strange sense of the predominance of cardboard.

In a wardrobe upstairs, front box room, I found some photographs in frames, no names, and the memories that could provide them − long gone. This frame here − I brought it down − let me measure it − it's so ornate that you know straight away what's in it is important and that is... a glass plate portrait of a very young child in petticoats. Now, this is a really early photograph. Got to the Valleys quickly, photography. Yes, studios everywhere as people poured in to the mines. Plenty of work to be had, and money to spend. Imagine it. The thrill. Seeing yourself in a photograph − for people who'd only ever had a mirror or a pail of water. You could even give yourself to your friends. You know, with a copy. On a *carte de visite,* they called them; the size of visiting cards the Quality used.

And you could capture change. This figure, now, in this photograph, is – well, like it was made of shadows. Insubstantial. And valuable. Quite an outlay to capture that fleeting stage, very early childhood. There he stands in his curls and petticoats. Within six months this little boy would've looked very different; a few years and a few more, and the photograph would be the only evidence of his short time in the world of women. But here's a strange thing: though the glass in the frame is intact, the thick photographic plate inside has been dealt a blow somehow. From a central point, it's cracked with this big starburst of fractures. The thin wooden board at the back's not in its original fixings. Someone, a long time ago, has tried to repair this, after some explosive bit of violence.

They were going to put it out with the rubbish here but I wouldn't let it go. I'm taking it home.

Which reminds me.... You do pick up the strangest things. You see what the family doesn't see.

I'll give you an instance. Here we are now in Briwnant Street but picture another house, not a million miles from here. A well-appointed Valleys house, eighteen-nineties, end-of-terrace, that bit bigger than its neighbours; the name BRYN ARIAN carved into its stone lintel. In Welsh that's 'Hill of Silver' – or 'of Money', depending. Its first owner was – I'd say – a poet. Or a miser.

This was back just before the Millennium that I was there. Winter. Probably November. Time was everywhere then. Countdown, run-up, apocalypse. End of the decade, of the century, of a decade of centuries. Bloody Robbie Williams wailing on about it on the radio: *mill-enny-UM, Da-daddy-da-da*. No escape.

Anyway. There I was, standing on my own in the back sitting-room of Bryn Arian: a nice high marble mantelpiece (not your common slate) and a mahogany sideboard facing it across the room. I won't have to tell you (because these houses are all of a type) that as I stood with my back to the mantelpiece I saw – over to the left, out through the open door – the banisters and panelling of stairs coming down into a hallway, and a bit of the black-and-white-tiled floor going up to a big, heavy front door with leaded lights. The furniture around me was extra respectable good stuff, and knew it. To my right was a solid square dining table covered in a thick chenille cloth that was weighed down all around with a heavy fringe. The table was almost as wide as the window it stood beneath. A cold light, I remember thinking, about that window. Cold.

I wasn't in Bryn Arian, mind you, because someone had died there. The son of the family had asked me to take a look at one particular thing: a hefty grandfather clock, before they got "you know – a *valuer* in". A proper expert, he meant. I said to him, "So it's your grandfather's clock, then." You know, little joke, little pun, like. But he just said, "That's right."

The clock stood to the left of the window. A lovely piece. Taller than a man. Bit of a giant grandfather. Locally made. Country scenes nicely painted in the four corners around the clock-face. All its weights and pendulum in good nick, hanging there behind the walnut door panel with the original crank key for winding it. In pencil on the inside of the door was a log of all the maintenance visits from the eighteen-seventies to nineteen-twelve. Done by a father and son, I'd say. *D. Abrahams* in a fancy hand and then, from nineteen-oh-one, the son's, neater: *Jacob*. Jewish immigrants, very likely. There was a faded business card – *Howells Jewellers* – from the nineteen-fifties pinned there with a tack. It's a firm that was in Ponty till about nineteen-eighty. All that time going by. All that careful attention.

And it was down inside the clock case, at the back, that I found the photograph. I nearly didn't, because there was just the tiniest corner visible, a crumb of white, peeping up from underneath the base plate. Tricky to get out. It was very late Victorian, not long before the First World War, and what they call a cabinet portrait. They're mounted on stiff card, a bit bigger than a postcard. It was a studio portrait of a young couple. Over-exposed. Fainter than it should have been. She's standing, he's sitting, surrounded by the photographer's props: little fake staircase, potted fern, fur rug, 'garden' backdrop. She's corseted and tense. There's something pleading in his expression.

So there I was, trying to work out if the two or three little rips and scores in it could be repaired. I put the photograph face-down on the table. The chenille was awkward, yielding and lumpy at the same time. And it trapped crumbs. In fact, I was surprised that, in such a self-assured household, this table-cloth hadn't been shaken out in ages. The crumbs and dust got in my way. Without something firm to lean on I couldn't get a purchase on the card and just as I was thinking it'd be tough to make anything stick, even if I'd had the right glue to hand, an elderly woman came in. Her white hair was pinned up in some way, elegant and efficient. She was about to go out by the look of her. A man her age – her husband, I supposed – drifted past in the background, down the hallway to the front door. She was the boss, she was. I picked that up straight away. It didn't suit her that I was there. When you work in other people's houses you get to know how they feel about you being in their space.

My interest in the photograph annoyed her – it wasn't what I was there for – but I was surprised she didn't ask me where I'd got it. I was going to put the obvious questions about who was in it and so on but she stopped me in my tracks by what she did come out with: if I'd be wanting 'more money for that'. No, no, I tell her, no need. Once she realised that me fiddling with the photograph wouldn't cost her anything she was mollified. And now she could dismiss it. It was my own time I was wasting. Still and all, as she left, I could tell she was irked that I'd noticed her reluctance to pay for anything she didn't have to.

So, I'm looking at the couple in the photo and then it strikes me: their clothes don't match. I mean, she's in her best black bodice and skirt, with a long string of jet beads and a gold watch chain on show but his suit's a working man's − far from a labourer's but the clothes of a man at work, not leisure.

I'm wondering why on earth it was in the clock − a thing like that doesn't get there by accident − somebody put it there; hid it there? − when the son comes in. He has an overcoat on. He's got these big, dark-brown eyes. Anxious. He sees I'm doing some-thing with the photograph, looks puzzled for a moment but asks me, politely enough, not, as I'd expected, about where the photo came from but what my credentials are for 'that kind of work'. I tell him I have no credentials, just my interest and careful attention and, I add (so he gets the point), my reputation.

I just get to tell him about finding the photo when this tall young woman comes along, his wife, and she wants him some-where else, that's obvious. She's dressed to go out too. She does no more than barely note me (and the old photo) but the way she speaks to him − as though I'm not there at all, you know − puts me in my place as not-one-of-them, more than if she'd told me bluntly that she's completely indifferent to me and anything I'm doing. Her coat falls open and I see that she's wearing a clerical collar and she is very, very pregnant. He hands me a brown enve-lope. Paper money inside. I say I'll leave a report. As they go out, he looks back at me, apologetic, like. He believes he has no choice.

And then he does turn back. I see him look for a second at the photograph I'm holding and he says that there were two of them. Two photographs, I say. No, he shakes his head, two clocks; identical almost, he'd heard. But his grandfather chopped one up.

Chopped...! I turn instinctively, protectively, to the clock. The *surviving* clock. The clock he could have touched if he'd reached out. Why, I ask, dead certain there must be an astonishing, an amazing, reason.

For firewood, he tells me.

I imagine the axe smashing into the polished wood. The clanging mangling of the chains. The glass shattering in the case. The wooden finials flying. The crumpling forward. For firewood! What sort of man...?

Surely if you were short of firewood, then sell the clock and buy as much as you wanted. No one destroys something so impressive and expensive without a good – or a powerful – reason.

While I'm gawping at the clock, he's gone. The front door shuts and I'm on my own. I got to admit I actually went up and stroked the clock, thinking of its twin − its companion? I even wondered what the clock felt to see one of its own – murdered.

I stand by that. I do. You see, a clock has a presence − is a presence − in a house. It's a living thing. It's got to be looked after, wound up, kept going.

Who cleared up afterwards – the shards of glass, the splinters? And when people noticed the clock was missing, how did they react to being told it had gone for firewood? Who decided that was a plausible reason for doing something so bizarre? Someone with a weak grip on normality, I'd say. But a strong grip. A strong grip on the family if they couldn't tell him how out of order he was.

He wouldn't even have had to say it himself. Someone else will have told the story. I imagine it being mentioned for the first time, in chapel, or in a shop. "The clock? Oh, firewood. It went for firewood." And the irrational is smoothed over, covered up. And so you're made to – how can I say it? – un-live what you lived. It didn't happen the way you experienced it. No, no. It went for firewood. You're made to live a lie and to hand it down into the future.

I stare at the photograph, at the clock. The photograph in the clock. The clock hiding it. Hiding it to protect it. From him. From the man with the axe, the householder, not the wistful young man in the photograph.

The clocks were older than the house. So they were brought here from somewhere else. One from the husband's family, one from the wife's? Was he attacking a person by means of a clock? Was he looking for something? Was he looking for the photograph and chose the wrong clock to break apart?

And the people in it: brother and sister? Husband and wife. Even, I find myself thinking, wife and young Jewish clock-maker? Yes, jewellers, clock-makers, often took to photography. Was it done in his studio, illicitly, hastily taken with someone's connivance, hence the under-exposure? While she, in her best clothes, waited for her husband to arrive for their joint portrait?

But I stop myself. Carried away. This family isn't asking, and it's their puzzle not mine. Yet I'm bent over that table troubling to repair their past! They don't care.

I leave the photograph where it is. I could tell them that I've seen the crumbs and the dust. Things are on the slide. I smell staleness and I feel how unsteady the air is here, disturbed by the flurry of their flight from things-as-they-are. To the people of this house it's even more urgent to escape the past, through hurrying on, hurrying out. What can have been so bad that it must be always run away from, turned away from, with all this hurrying into a future that recedes as fast as it's chased?

I could have told them that I hear what the photograph whispers: *As I am so will you be.* There's a message for you, now. A message they don't want to hear. No more than they can bear to think of all the un-lived life among the lives of those who've gone before them. I think about that. You can be made to deny stuff that actually happened, so how can you ever tell what's really going on? That's confusing. Big time. You never know where you are, so you just keep going. These people, this family in Bryn Arian, they have cars to start and sermons to give and so they believe they're going somewhere else – and not where the people in the photograph went. They believe themselves to be alive.

But Death, now. People like these refuse to let Death take root in their lives. You might say, but the young pregnant wife was a priest. She must have been dealing with Death more than most; taking funerals, burying the dead. But I got her number. Just because you can slot Death in at the crem. doesn't mean you're controlling him, but it might encourage you to think you were. Am I right? Bossing Death about, like a relative nobody likes. The awkward uncle you keep shunting around the family. That's just one way of trying to keep him from settling in. Other people simply refuse to see him. They talk across him or they treat him like any other burden, a dull companion on the sofa, to be borne with but never really attended to. But I know different, see. I know Death prefers to make an entrance early, to season each year with a particular tang, to grow as we grow, to get us used to loss and letting go.

Death's our friend. He is. Really. He strains and expands our tight little dreams till they burst like... seedpods. Pfff! He takes us to a vantage-point – the end of the year, an illness, a crisis – and there he whispers, hot and close in the ear, "Enough for you, is it, what you see back there behind you? Is that all there's going to be?"

And Death, our enemy, yeah, he goads us, wants us to put up a fight, to turn and face him and learn from our defeats – those times we let Death get the upper hand, when we didn't keep hold of Life. Death wants a worthy opponent, not someone who's half his from the start, like the man who tolerated that hideous, bilious quilt upstairs here in Briwnant Street.

But at least here there's only a sense of defeat. Back there in Bryn Arian what got to me was a wilful refusal to acknowledge the fight. Death doesn't like that. After all, he's the great expert in Time and he likes the stakes to be high. He wants us to look back, to fear the waste of Time. He doesn't want to be cheated of our regret, our remorse, our real mucked-up life. He doesn't want only to be directed to the nice stuff.

Death, by the way, does like clocks. They allow him a moment of drama. Death, the great clock-stopper. Ta-da! Anyone who murders a clock, that wouldn't go down well with Death because when there's no Time to stop, Death is redundant, upstaged.

Well, I took a last look at that grandfather clock, then I left a note and I left the money too. I despised them all. I put the note on the table beside that photograph. 'Irreparable', the note said.

But, before I turned away from Bryn Arian, a pang of pity halted me and also, you know, fair play, I thought. I should try to be accurate and fair – professional, like. The son – the grandson – did tell me about the second clock and he did give me the crazy justification about the firewood. Was that his bid for freedom? A hope that at long last someone else's outrage will break the spell?

So, I thought, where there's life, there's time. Maybe.

I added to the note the words, 'by me'.

'Irreparable by me.'

AN ULSTER PSYCHE

I was shocked by her photographs. How could she dare? As well as projected slides she had a dozen cibachromes on display whose marvellously luminous surface makes the paper itself a fresh lens. It becomes a pool of water in which everything is gently enhanced by the limpid medium. And yet, this pool is pinned to a wall.

I had to leave the room. Such things should not be shown without a warning.

Or, I thought, once outside in the corridor, perhaps they need, not a warning, but a ritual to precede them. She wouldn't know this. That was it, most likely.

I considered her a beautiful-looking woman, with a detachment from her appearance which is rare these days. She didn't know she was beautiful. She saw and photographed beauty in the natural world with flair, as a labour of love, with a willingness to invest long hours of hard waiting, in frost or in water, to catch the moment that blesses the subject with just the conjunction of light and attention that quickens its core; like those December solstice mornings when the dying sun labours to the top of a standing stone outside a megalith. Its rays, though weak, are straight, and human ingenuity harnessed them long ago by a slot above the sealed door of the tomb. They have no choice but to travel deeper in, between the massive incised slabs that line the passage, and strike the back wall, flooding the grave with light. She had learnt how to perceive and receive such an instant of revelation and present it to us in a photograph.

How had she learnt? How could someone like her learn? No, not that. More precisely: how could someone like her learn to notice and record things that were ours, not hers; things that we would never have discussed in front of people like her.

She came from a townland whose name, I knew, means the Ford of the Sand Dunes. But she didn't know that. Families like hers worked fields whose names conveyed nothing to them. Irish is seen as a completely useless and alien language and ignorance of it as not only normal but justified by its economic irrelevance. They think it an unenlightened language, in league with the forces of Romanist repression and dark superstition.

She'd told me that as a child she and her siblings spent many Sunday afternoons in car parks, on beach-fronts or grassy plots, listening to her father and other members of their gospel hall witnessing to the saving power of the Lord Jesus Christ. He had not lain in the tomb waiting for a creature like the sun to warm him into life. He burst the bands and emerged in his own blaze. They were God-fearing, bible-believing Christians who hung texts on their walls and stood firm against art.

Art, then, had been her ray of sunlight! Yes. It had only needed a chink and it got in. And she was lost. Her father said so. Her mother pleaded. She went to university and, as they had feared, encountered Catholics. Not too close an encounter, mind you. Perhaps one of them had told her about a shrine by a puddle of a well or rags tied to a tree. Going to such places had been enough to lead her even further back

I paced the corridor. It was not her problem. It was mine. The innocent can stray unharmed where the guilty dare not go. Should I tell her? Wouldn't that be to place a burden on her shoulders, making her uncomfortably conscious of what she had done? Her own beauty, carried without egotism, moved the shadows quietly aside. Let her work go on, then, disturbing our depths as none of us would have dared. Perhaps it was fated. Psyche lifts her lamp.

That resolution lasted till I re-entered the room. Some Americans were saying crass things about her photographs. I told myself repeatedly that art is human and that all human response is valid. I sat very still. Psyche, I told myself, lifts her lamp to see the one who has captured her heart. That's all each of us here is doing. We've encountered something beautiful and we lift up our responses to see more clearly. The fact that these Americans have arrived in the sanctuary with a ghetto-blaster shouldn't matter. If that helps them see, far be it from me.... It was no use! My heart was tearing as I heard them. Psyche lifts her lamp and drops of hot oil fall searingly on Love's skin. He wakes and flies away because she has looked on him too soon, with too crude a curiosity.

I would have to buy some of these photographs, to rescue just a few for her and make sure that they received the reverence they deserved.

It took me a while to get the money together and longer still after that to track her down because she moved often, passing from one continent to another. In the meantime, I had those images in my head.

She had worked with disc-shaped mirrors, about a foot across. These she placed in the open where they would catch images of what passed over them. In one series, she photographed ten of them on the crimped sand left by a retreating tide. Where all was shifting, either on the strand or in the sky, the mirrors' sharp circumferences caught – like bowls – an image, each one different to the next. The photograph, by fixing the instant, spoke to us of change.

For another set of pictures she had climbed for a whole day, carrying mirrors in a rucksack, to get to a corry lake, pooled darkly at the feet of precipitous, scrubby slopes. These were the images that most disturbed me. One could not go to such a place unprepared. And yet she had. And returned unharmed.

These lakes contain no light. The sun penetrates a few surface inches and is baulked. Peat darkens the water. The wind raises superficial ripples but nothing disturbs the depths. Something down there is unmoved by us. Our agitations and passions are nullified. We look into them and see – nothing. A subtle shock. A shift behind the breast-bone. A glimpse of the silence – the darkness – of the moment of death.

Our technique for dealing with this is not a secret. It used to be gold and silver, whatever was hardest won and least replaceable. The precious things were thrown from a height into the water: swords, jewellery, pots and knives. Things that carry light in themselves. The smith struck sparks as he beat the blade. He made light from metal. What power, then, what self-assertion, to fling a thing like that into the blackness, knowing it could never be retrieved and, rather than be undermined by the threat of loss, to deprive ourselves willingly.

Later it was indeed our selves we threw. That heavy power that squatted, indifferent to us, in barracks, ministries or law-courts was like these lakes. It swallowed up a language, a culture, a future. We pitied it contemptuously and let ourselves grow thin. We nourished instead a talent for endurance, a sardonic patience, and a reverence for suffering as an act of war.

Meanwhile her people prospered, in a thrifty style. Pebble-dash, modest flower beds, pastel outfits, well-filled suits. Plenty of light. Was that it? She went up there and put a mirror into the water. She waited. The sun found it. She clicked the shutter.

Weeping and wailing! There should be cries and ululations! A golden sun in the water! Are the gods spitting out all we have given up?

At last I found her, on an island. A cold, brash sea drives a hard bargain around that place. Storey upon storey of sea-birds conduct their business on the cliffs. This little world stands off from the mainland, like a dealer at a fair inspecting from the edge of the crowd, suspending judgement.

She was startled. Her man suspicious. No one had shown interest in those photographs. I had to wait another year because they could not be found.

I have them now. But the ones I bought show the moon, snared by a mirror placed among shale, and those taken on the beach: inversions. The heights brought down. I could not bring myself to acquire the lake shots – the depths brought up? No. That hadn't happened. The gods would not punish her for sacrilege. She acted according to her tribe when, seeing darkness, she put in light. All the deeper is the realm that she couldn't reach, the unbought photograph said, and those hidden presences smiled.

I honour the version my imagination keeps. And I honour her for seeking her beloved, who, in this country, has not 'gone down to the beds of spices, to pasture his flock in the gardens' but hid himself, long ago, in the darkest places of the land. She must have sensed his presence there and 'done what she could', wanting the sun to enter the tomb.

Preacher-father, you need us. You are too clean and your Christ too efficient but your daughter has done the one essential thing. Sitting at his feet among the sand-dunes, she has seen his other face, the one we glimpse and know: the one who fails to make a difference, who is irrelevant, yesterday's man. Your daughter is a ford. You and I can cross, changing places, feeling the ground shift beneath our feet. I need your steadying hand.

MERCY

Francie entered the house as quietly as possible, from the back. He crossed the small kitchen stealthily. He wanted to catch Jim alone, without Seamie's nurse around or any of the family. He knew their mother was likely to be in the sickroom at this point in the afternoon. A few steps took him to the door of the front sitting-room. It was ajar. Jim stood in there, facing the picture window, a makeshift drawing-board propped on his waist, a pencil between his fingers. Francie glimpsed the sketch: his brother's own face, frowning in self-criticism. Was that a good or a bad omen? Whichever, they had to talk today. Francie was determined. There was so little time left. At a noise from upstairs – an elderly cough, chesty and laboured – Francie saw Jim's pencil instantly halt on the paper and his body tense with irritation.

Francie swiftly considered his tactics.

"It's yourself," he called out buoyantly as he pushed the door wide and went in.

Instantly he regretted his choice as Jim put the drawing brusquely aside, crumpling it briefly and quashing Francie's curiosity about it with an abrupt, "It's nothing." He gave Francie his attention with a calm hostility but Francie had come prepared this time. He pulled out a pack of photographs and opened it.

"Look! These are from last Saturday over at Ballygall. Doesn't Pearse's place look grand? All five of us and Mammy, and – ach! I've given up counting the kids – and the four wives. Micky's Mary is expecting again. There should be a grant for being an uncle – bloody Christening presents, eh? You're smiling in this one, Jim. The oul fella'll be pleased."

"That I'm smiling?" Jim said drily.

"That there's a good one of us all," Francie replied patiently. He handed the pack to Jim who went through them with attention but little reaction.

Francie watched him: the sort of non-response he'd expected. Still, never say die. Jim had grown thin – a physique like a teenager's though he was well into his thirties – and touchy too. Had he always been like this? Francie struggled to remember. Couldn't. He had barely started school when Jim left home. He'd ask Pearse, or better still, Pearse's wife, who had known the family so long that she'd be able to tell him and she wouldn't be defensive.

Poor bugger, thought Francie, as he watched Jim. What was the point in being good-looking if you were locked inside…. He found himself scrutinised as Jim looked up at him. Francie leapt to Jim's side.

"There! That's the one," Francie said.

"Obviously," Jim replied tersely.

They looked at a group shot of five young men, including themselves. Each, apart from Jim, stood with a woman. Their mother, Maura, at the centre of the group, looked pleased but tense, as though she were on the verge of going inside the handsome house visible in the lawned background, to cry discreetly and briefly.

"Wouldn't he have loved to've been there?" sighed Francie. Jim glanced askance at him. "A bit of craic and a drink or several," Francie smiled.

"Loved it if he could've been the centre of attention," Jim corrected him.

"Well, he would have been! His ruby wedding, after all!" He took the photos from Jim who, he told himself, had probably always been an awkward bastard – like the oul' fella himself. He peeled off a photo and placed it on the mantelpiece, pointedly not offering it to Jim. "I'll leave that there for you. I have the negatives."

Jim said nothing, turning to the window that framed the nondescript garden, its hedge bordering the street of modest semis where the five brothers had grown up. And what was there new to see out there, Francie wondered. Republican West Belfast, same flags on the lamp-posts on a Monday as a Tuesday; same slogans daubed up: I.RA., Provos or Sinn Féin. Jim was a bit of a negative himself, mind, in those white shirts and black trousers he always wore. Poor bugger, Francie thought again.

"How long have you got, Jim?" he asked sympathetically.

"I have leave to stay till... the end."

"Tough on you, being here all the time. Would you not stay with me and Aileen?"

"I can't. And it's any day now." They were both silent.

"A cup of tea!" said Francie, berating himself even as he left the room for taking such an obvious escape route.

Jim considered the familiar hedge – half a stone's throw. No, just a little more. An army foot patrol approached. Twenty-four years – two-thirds of his own life – since they had first arrived in nineteen-sixty-nine. An ungainly, strung-out caterpillar they were, as they lumbered along the pavement in their greenish camouflage. To fit in round here they'd be better off wearing brick red and the grey of metal fencing with a flecking of barbed wire. Squawking, the creepy-crawly kept in touch with its nest via bursts of static. Jim looked away. He did not want to meet any eyes. He did not want them to see he was attracted to what he hated and that he admired that discipline, that unity of purpose, that not shirking the thankless, plodding routine for the sake of the great goal. Like a higher species, a helicopter droned overhead, its whirring blades a threat of punishment.

Jim winced. Like the oul' fella. Yes, his approach too had always been heralded by a shift in the air, a displacement of the normal currents.

Jim stood, again a teenager, at this window, with the household sounds around him: his brothers careering around the cramped house, his mother in the kitchen with the hit of nineteen-seventy-four on the radio: *Sugar Baby Love, Sugar Baby Love... I didn't mean to make you cry...* The music bounced and jangled. Jim, like a lookout, called, "He's coming!" Instantly the radio was silenced. His brothers scuttled downstairs. He knew his mother would be crushing her cigarette into the sink and putting her apron back on and Pearse would be re-folding the paper to make it look as though it hadn't been read. As their father turned in at the gate, homework books were spread out, expressions assumed. As he came up the path he noticed Jim and blinked in instinctive self-defence. He frowned and pulled out a key. "Hello, Seamie!" Jim heard his mother say brightly as the door opened.

"I've put the kettle on," Francie announced, returning. There was no response. "I had a long talk with him," he said eventually. Jim was startled. "On our own. Yesterday. You were busy with the... eh... high-up who came to see you... so it was easier. Well, Daddy always had a soft spot for me. Poor oul' sod."

Francie, realising he would be given no further opening, picked up the drawing, playing for time. He tugged the paper flat. "It's you to the life! Bloody marvellous. Though I hope you don't feel as bad as you look here! Do you remember the times he tried to teach *me* to draw? 'Look, boy! You're not looking. You won't draw if you don't look!' And the day he had us all out painting a mural on the back wall and we ran out of paint and then we ran out on him! And taking us to art galleries. You were the only one who was really interested, I always heard. There were drawings of yours knocking around the house, well, up in the attic, for ages. Ah, no. It can't have been easy for him. I've only the one kid myself and I'm driven distracted."

"He got off to work, didn't he?" Jim countered grudgingly.

"But," said Francie carefully. "it was just slog, to pay the bills. He hated it. Work all day. Then home to us." He put on an irate voice. "'Can I not have peace in my own house?' Remember?"

"I don't forget," Jim said tersely.

"I know it was hard, the tension, the not-putting-a-foot-wrong...."

"You were too young for the worst of it!"

"Am I supposed to be sorry about that? I can't help being the youngest."

"It was different for you."

"Was it?" Francie waited.

"We'd sit there," Jim said suddenly, "while he read the paper. We'd be longing to get away. I used to watch him. 'Give over, you!' he said to me one time. 'You're like the avenging angel!' And Liam whispers to me, 'What's the avenging angel?' The paper rustled. He didn't like that. No. Any minute...!"

"Any minute...?" Francie prompted.

"And then you ran in, three years old, bright as a button: 'Daddy!' And I swear he smiled at you. Couldn't help himself. And you rushed up to hug him. But he saw me watching him.

Yeah. So, well, then he had to push you away, didn't he, and you trying to climb on his knee and you fell off and, oh, big tears! Up he gets, pushing you with his foot and roaring, 'Can I not have peace in my own house?' And I grabbed you up and I yelled at him, 'Leave Francie alone! Leave us all alone!' He gawped at me, holding his own child away from him, and he tried to get you, but I wouldn't move an inch. He stepped back and his knees were against the sofa and... he was on his arse! Looking up at me. In front of all of you! So I bloody dropped you and ran!"

Jim was short of breath. Francie tried to imagine that running. "Where did you go?"

"What?" Jim asked distractedly.

"Where did you run to?" Jim turned away and did not answer. "Look, Jim," Francie ventured, "I don't remember that and if I don't...." He hesitated. "Maybe you shouldn't."

"Why shouldn't...?"

"We've all done things to spite him. No artists in this family. I'm in Weights and Measures, for God's sake! Micky (God bless him) a barman. Pearse an accountant. We have a teacher and *you....*"

"Yes!" Jim said quickly. "I've been away a long time... a long time. I wanted to be as unlike him as I could possibly be. I wanted to do something...; to give... something...." He turned, this way and that. He went to the mantelpiece, picked up the photograph and looked hard at it. He said, as though expecting to be challenged, "Well, there are things I want, now." Francie gazed at him, perplexed. "Anything is possible if you feel it's right; but if you begin to see you've decided for the wrong reasons...." He stopped.

"Are you saying...?"

Jim spoke, head down, his voice stiff with emotion, "There's no bearing it, is what I'm saying."

"What are you…?" Francie began and then, with a start of shocked perception, he gasped, "You want out!"

Jim could hear Francie's anxiety: the perplexed exhalation, the shifting stance. Francie would be rapidly calculating the appalling consequences, the shame, the mess.

"Oh, God. Oh, my God," Francie whispered at last. "Will they let you go? Aren't you in for life?" Jim looked away. "You're so like him!" Francie, burst out. He tried to keep his voice down. "So bloody all or nothing! Look at you!" He thrust out Jim's drawing but Jim ignored it. Francie quelled the urge to shake his silent brother. That would only increase the resistance he'd come to tackle. Another bout of coughing from overhead decided him. He would deal with the immediate issue. "Jim," he began quietly. "Did you hear that? He's not the man he was. Is he? He's lying up there.... You and he could talk...."

"You're all stuffing the past in another room like it never happened! How can you talk to someone who doesn't ever admit there was anything wrong? Who never looks at me!"

"Never looks...?" Francie repeated, aware of a pang of compassion.

There was a disturbance overhead and their mother's urgent cry, "Jim! Quick! Jim!" Francie instantly dashed out, still holding the drawing. A heavy slump shuddered the ceiling. Jim heard his mother's surprised, "Francie!" There was a burst of dreadful coughing. When Jim got to the door of the bedroom, his father was wailing, "You all go!" Francie answered mildly, "Sure where would we be going?" as he settled Seamie on the bed, adding jovially, "You're putting on weight! I'll soon not be able to lift you – and you always such a trim man."

A helicopter groaned low over the house and away as Jim entered but Francie halted him by saying, coolly, "No need. I managed." He obliged Jim to step back over the threshold and closed the door of the bedroom behind both of them. "I'm keeping what you've told me to myself," he whispered. "You know what I think you should do and you should do it today."

That night Jim sat by the foot of Seamie's bed as Maura prayed the rosary aloud with her eyes closed: "Hail, Mary, full of grace, the Lord is with thee...." Her voice was incantatory after dozens of repetitions. Jim gazed at the fake candle-flame above her head: a torpedo-shaped red bulb attached to the wall. It looked to him like an elongated, livid bullet. It glowed before a picture of the Sacred Heart of Jesus. All his life he had seen that image in so many homes, familiar to the point of invisibility: Jesus revealing his heart from among the folds of his garment, 'all burning with fervent love for men' – the sweet-melodied hymn recurred to Jim, redolent of fervent, sombre devotions and humble, often senti-mental, piety. "Holy Mary," Jim responded, "Mother of God, pray for us now and at the hour of our death. Amen."

Maura's rosary beads shifted between her fingers – needlessly, Jim thought, irritated, hearing her stretch out the chain of beads, then trickle them down into one hand before repeating the action time and again. He longed to be somewhere else. He glared at the paraphernalia of sickness: the useless medicines, the oxygen cylin-der, and the scurf of tissues, unread newspapers and pill packets. A heavy wristwatch nestled among them – too heavy for the man in the bed ever to wear again. His mother had never liked house-work. She had relaxed the routine that had been imposed and policed by Seamie.

"Hail, Mary, full of grace..." she recited. Jim closed his eyes in an effort to block his irritation. "Blessed art thou among women..." Maura continued.

"Holy Mary, Mother of God," Jim began, opening his eyes at random. He was shocked to see Seamie pulling out from among the bedclothes the sketch of himself he had made that morning. Automatically, he continued the response.

While Maura prayed on, unaware, Seamie gestured with the drawing, feebly, in his son's direction. Jim bristled. Seamie made an effort to nod approvingly towards the drawing and in his eyes Jim saw an attempt at praise.

"Blessed art thou amongst women..." Maura intoned. Seamie reached out with the drawing towards Jim. Seamie was pleading now, silently, trying to smile. Jim's voice, in the response, hardened. He made no move.

"Pray for us now," Jim said, "and at the hour of our death. Amen."

Seamie groaned and subsided. Maura opened her eyes and saw him trying to speak. "What, love?" she asked solicitously, bending to catch and repeat his mumbled words. "'You can't wait'? Who can't, Seamie?" She glanced at Jim and wondered at his hostile expression. Seamie, looking hard at Jim, rasped with effort, "You can't wait... for the hour...."

"Oh, now...!" Maura broke in, suddenly apprehensive, as Seamie struggled to say, "of my...." But his breath failed him and Maura saw Jim lock eyes with his father and say to him, implacably, "of your death." Seamie held his gaze in mute acknowledgement.

"Jim!" cried Maura, appalled, but father and son were focused on each other. The drawing slid off the bed onto the floor. Jim began the final prayer, never taking his eyes from Seamie's face. "Glory be to the Father, and to the Son, and to the Holy Spirit...." Seamie was gripped by a spasm of coughing. Maura leapt to raise him in the bed. Jim supplied her response, "as it was in the beginning, is now, and ever shall be...." Maura, her own body shaken by Seamie's struggle, twisted towards Jim in appeal. "Amen," Jim insisted, ignoring her beseeching eyes.

Less than a week later Francie stood shivering in the cemetery. Autumn sunlight, bright but frail, picked out the mica flecks in a grave-kerb by his feet, sprinkling it with tiny glistenings. Someone was fretting: Pearse. He was muttering about the grave's location; how it shouldn't have been half-way down the sloping site but in the higher, drier ground; how they could have afforded a prestige position if they'd got their act together. Francie ignored him and moved towards his mother. She was not a woman who drew other women to her, even in these circumstances. Her daughters-in-law kept a distance, knowing that she wouldn't welcome the physical-ity that was second nature to them: the arm around the shoulders, the caresses, actual or murmured.

As he reached her, a neighbour woman was tentatively patting her sleeve. "Maura, Maura. Haven't you the fine sons to remember him by!" Were they fine, Francie wondered. How much support had they given her? Perhaps he himself was guilty of taking her for granted, of never encouraging her to do anything but drift in Seamie's wake, letting her manage him by stealth so that the rest of them could avoid his irritability. As the youngest, he had been buffered by his brothers; and his easy-going nature meant he could get the oul' fella to laugh now and then, even on the sacred topic of his talent. Maura stuck to the script, of Seamie as the father who had sacrificed his artistic ambitions for the sake of the family: the Great Could-Have-Been. Maybe they'd all accepted that too readily, for an easy life. If Seamie had really wanted to, couldn't he have found some kind of art to do? Why had it been so stark a choice? Only Jim had resisted the party line, implacably. But perhaps that was easier from a distance.

"Gracious Lord, forgive the sins of those who have died in Christ. Lord in your mercy...."

Francie tried to pay attention to the words of the committal service.

"Hear our prayer," the mourners responded.

Seamie's death had not come easily but in exhausting bouts that he had fought like an out-classed old boxer entering the ring time and again. Francie had sweated, having to watch. At last he had bent down and whispered in his father's ear, "Daddy, it's all right to let go now." He had seen relief and gratitude in Seamie's eyes but then their gaze had moved, just a little, and hardened defiantly, losing that peace. Francie had turned on the instant, protective against whatever had provoked this pathetic stand, and found Jim at the foot of the bed.

Francie brushed past Jim now where he stood by the undertakers while they prepared to transfer Seamie's coffin to the shoulders of four of his sons. Francie was glad, as he put his arm around Micky's shoulder, feeling Pearse and Liam heft the casket behind them, that he didn't have to wrestle with how he'd feel if it had been Jim beside him, bearing Seamie the final few yards. But this was worse, he thought as, ahead, he saw the sunlight catching the little gold cross sewn on each end of the thin purple stole that Jim wore over his black clerical suit.

Jim turned the page of the heavy service book although he hardly needed to read the prayers, so well did he know them, "Welcome him to eternal life. Lord, in your mercy...."

"Hear our prayer."

Francie looked at his brother, the priest. "Let us also pray for ourselves on our pilgrimage through life," he heard him say. "Keep us faithful in your service."

Seamie had faithfully worked to keep the family, Francie reflected, but with an embittered doggedness. There was often a sourness about him that set people on edge. He spoke up. He spoke out. Had they all, to one extent or another, compensated for that frustration by letting him dominate at home? Had it been collusion and not love?

Swaying a little under the burden, Francie reached the graveside with his brothers. The very end of his father's life. A time for honesty, surely. He had little doubt that each of them was thinking the same thing: that one day it would be their turn to be the father carried to the grave, his life assessed and the sons assessing their own. Francie confessed to himself that he had not loved his father as much as he could have. He had presented him with a front and, he'd have to say, they all did. Their lives – his mother's, his brothers' – had gone on in an area they kept him out of.

The four brothers set the coffin carefully down on the straps laid ready, took these up, braced themselves to the weight and lowered the coffin into the grave. An undertaker motioned to Pearse and to Micky to pull a strap-end each. Both of them looked uncomprehendingly at the man until Micky, with a jerk of his head, said, "Oh, aye!" rather comically and nodded to Pearse while gesturing to him with the strap. Flushing with embarrassment, Pearse tugged his strap with such energy that it rattled alarmingly under the coffin and up the side of the grave, emerging with a heavy flap. The word 'fish' was muttered disparagingly. Pearse scowled.

Jim announced a decade of the rosary and during its recitation the mourners, one by one, threw a pinch of earth into the grave, some pausing to murmur a few words, or bless themselves before filing on. The younger children gazed with frank interest into the hole, straining out from their parents' grip. Jim approached last.

Holding the service book clasped against his chest, he tossed some earth into the grave but remained there, looking in over the edge. He didn't move. Everyone waited, to the point where they became uneasy.

Pearse acted. He stepped up beside Jim and looked into the grave. He saw nothing amiss and, wanting to move things on in some unobtrusive way, assumed a sombre voice and read out the inscription on the coffin. "Seamus Joseph Caraher. Twenty-fourth of September, nineteen-nineteen to the tenth of October, nineteen-ninety-three."

Micky joined him, looking down at the brass plaque. He said to Jim, "He liked the Sacred Heart. So we put it on his coffin. We asked you. Remember? We didn't put a crucifix as well because we reckoned the Heart was enough." Getting no response, he persisted. "I mean, it's the same guy – heart or crucif...."

"Micky!" Pearse snapped.

Micky sniffed, sure of his ground. He read from the coffin-lid, "'Sacred Heart of Jesus, I place all my trust in thee.'" He shrugged as though to say, case proved.

Suddenly, Jim opened the book and read with urgent difficulty, "God of holiness and power accept our prayers on behalf of your servant, Seamus Joseph. Do not count his deeds against him...." He paused. He was struggling with emotion. Liam put a sympathetic hand on his shoulder but it was shrugged brusquely away. "Do not count his deeds against him..." Jim repeated, "for in his heart.... in his heart...."

Was Jim about to collapse, Francie wondered. But even as Francie moved towards him, Jim let the book drop and swung round so abruptly that the crowd parted before him, startled. An action of such conviction must somehow be part of the ceremony, surely, but as they watched Jim stride away between the graves the mourners realised there would be no satisfying twist, restoring order, edifying all. They began to huddle and whisper together.

Pearse turned on Francie furiously as the murmuring turned to outright questioning. Gesturing to the brothers to stay put, Francie ran after Jim, caught up with him and held his arm. Jim shook him off, demanding, "You know what it says?"

Francie was at a loss. "'Do not count his deeds against him!'" Jim urged.Seeing no comprehension, he laughed harshly. "'For in his heart he desired to do your will.' In his heart! It doesn't matter what harm he actually did because he didn't want to do it really – not in his heart. So let him into heaven. We'll call it quits!" He shook his head, "I won't have it!" and plunged away.

Francie saw his brothers bearing down on them. He ran back towards them. "Overcome with grief," he insisted, facing down their outrage. "Take everyone on to the meal. I'll deal with him," he said.

"You'd bloody better!" Pearse snarled.

Francie watched from a distance, standing by a clump of scraggy bushes in the very lowest part of the cemetery. Jim was sitting on a grave kerb, occasionally flinging a pebble viciously against a headstone. At last Francie went forward.

"Jim," he said quietly. Jim looked up. He was suffering. Francie was encouraged. Better that than stubborn indignation. He sat down beside his brother. "Jim," Francie began, "don't stay here. Come back with the rest of us."

Jim turned roughly away.

"Jim, he's dead. Dead and...."

"Forgiven!"

"Well... yes. Of course, he's...."

"Escaped!" Jim's face contorted.

An instinctive recoil prickled through Francie. There was something powerful here and he wasn't sure he could handle it.

"I wanted him punished!" Jim swung towards a stone crucifix carved on a memorial. "So fucking merciful!" he hissed at the pinioned figure on it. "It's never too late with you, is it? Well, I'm not you. I won't be you!"

"Who's asking you to be...?"

Jim was incredulous. "That's who I ought to be. It doesn't make sense otherwise. 'All or nothing.' But I can't give 'all'. I've tried. I could cope while I had a reason but now he's gone... and forgiven..." Jim paused, his eyes blank with horror, "There's no one left to blame but me."

"Blame you for what, Jim?"

"A thing...."

"What thing?"

"A good thing...."

"Yes?"

"A good thing... for a bad reason."

"Jim. What have you done?" Francie waited, dreading to know.

"That time I ran away...."

"Yes?"

"That time I ran away I ended up in the church. At least I could be quiet there. I sat – I hid – at the Sacred Heart altar. There were red flowers all over: roses, gladioli... stiff like spears... carnations, pinks; perfume, and heat from the candles; the mosaic – that dull-gold mosaic – smouldering, almost, as it got darker and darker. There He was up there, showing his heart, with flames around it, burning. A burning heart. Mine was burning – with rage and shame and not being able to *do* anything... not change anything. I was seventeen. There was no peace in our house. Why did he drive us all the time? And it was all false and nobody would say.

I sat there, looking. It was all redness and shadows. Like a womb. I thought: I could love. I could. I could paint a better Sacred Heart than that, more real, more like someone you could meet and love, not this mawkish, womanish eunuch. I could paint! I could love!"

Francie waited.

"Father Maurice found me," Jim went on. "He was kind. He persuaded me to come home. 'I'll talk to your father.' He said things would be all right."

"Were they?"

"Oh, he listened to Father Maurice's little go-easy-on-him speech and he said, 'Yes' and 'No' and 'Good night' But as soon as the door was closed he pinned me against the wall. 'You go running to the priests? I'm your father. I'm your father!' I smiled, and at that he banged me off the wall until Mammy was scream-ing. I could hear myself thinking: 'You're not. You're not.'"

Francie was appalled "But this good thing you did that was so bad?" he prompted.

"Somehow, at some point – I don't remember when – I don't remember how... maybe I saw... that I *could* get away, and every-one would praise me and he'd not be able to contradict them, for what better thing could a son do?"

It was several moments before Francie could trust himself to speak.

"A priest," he stated flatly.

"I'd get a new family, a greater ideal, greater than his – his art. I'd give up everything. He was the great renouncer, wasn't he? But not compared to me!"

Francie watched Jim cradle his right fist in his left hand, turn-ing the one inside the other, grinding. Abruptly the fingers interlaced in the clasp of prayer and Jim unthinkingly brought them to his mouth. He rubbed his teeth over the knuckle of his thumb, his thoughts elsewhere as the skin reddened.

Francie looked round for his brothers, for anyone. The boggy land rumpled between graves. Tufts of scruffy rushes suggested a footing but were only a crust, Francie knew. He'd spent many an hour playing here, aware of being on the surface, while underground another kind of life was busying itself.

Francie shifted position a little. "Nobody made you be a priest. You must have wanted it, Jim. It's not like getting married – one big day and you're tied for life – you had years to reflect, to choose differently. And you chose not simply to be a priest but to join a religious order. You didn't have to do that."

Francie was surprised when Jim nodded, though still hunched. "I was happy actually. Yes. I was. They were glad to have me. I thought I'd found a family. But then, after I was ordained, when I was supposed to have grown up, I understood that most of them were only muddling through too. You weren't supposed to be lonely. The lonely came to you for advice. You couldn't be lonely. One time I went to the Superior's room – his own room, his bedroom, you know – to hand in the final draft of a report he'd been chasing me for and as I got near the door I could hear him inside, crying. Should I knock? Should I help? I thought, yes. He's supposed to be my brother and I knocked, ready to share, but he opened the door, breezy and bluff as ever, though I could see a tear still on his chin that he hadn't wiped away. And he said, no, no problem, took the papers off me and shut the door. You see? There was no escape. If he had to lock himself away, then so did I. There was no escape from our solitary selves. No quarter. No mercy."

Francie put an arm around Jim and stroked his hair, as he would his own small son's, and he felt Jim's head making a child's response, a blind nuzzling into the collar bone, a slow turning of the head from side to side, pressing the brow into Francie's shoulder as though saying no, no, till, gradually, the movement ceased and Francie felt a sigh escape. A final moment of stillness and Jim pulled back, wiping his face, breathing in deeply then exhaling.

"I killed him," Jim said at last. "You saw. More than once I did it. I had his talent and I killed that in myself. And I made him watch. I enjoyed being able to say piously that I wouldn't be painting again. The Order didn't demand that. It was self-imposed. He had to listen and have people congratulating him – such a fine son."

"No wonder you've been unhappy," said Francie, trying to keep the revulsion out of his voice.

Jim met his gaze. He said, eventually, calmly, even nobly, "I've only myself to blame."

Francie let this stand and then took Jim by the upper arms and spoke very slowly, emphasising each word, "You… fucking… liar." A helicopter groaned into earshot and hovered, roaring, over-head. It was pointless trying to speak. Francie held Jim in place till it passed, then tugged him to his feet. "You know that's not true," he insisted. "Nobody's perfect. Nobody's perfectly to blame. Get down here with the rest of us!" Jim was stunned. "Jesus Christ! Who do you think you are?" Francie went on. "You did your *bit* to kill him. That's *all*!"

Francie pushed Jim away and left him. But just before he disappeared over a lift in the land, he stopped. An impulse of pity, for Jim, for Seamie, for all of them, made him turn and call out, "At least be a priest for him now."

Wooden boards had been placed across the unfilled grave and mats of green plastic grass spread over twin mounds of excavated earth on each side. The funeral flowers lay precariously on these. Several had slid and lay askew. Jim raised his hand in blessing over Seamie but could not speak. "God sees me," he said to himself.

"He knows my heart." That thought – its instant, humbling pain – prised him further open.

At the cemetery gates, Jim paused and looked back. In the distance, the helicopter was a dragonfly, whirring in a high, powdery, sky. The tall celtic crosses, white and buff and grey, clustered like massive sedge-plants, huge and bulky-headed, on the edge of the slope leading down to the Bog Meadows. He could see a pattern in it. Chalk on pale blue paper.

KINSHIP

The consultant is a peppery little man. Likes short answers. 'Yes' and 'No', preferably. But I'm not finding it easy to distil, out of years of symptoms, a one-word answer for him. He's irascible, peremptory – yes, peremptory. Exactly that. Little parps and beeps of irritation emerge from him. Does he dislike sick people? "Bend forward," he says to me. "Bend backwards. Now to the side. And to the other. Go into that cubicle. I shall be back in one moment."

Or is it just Irish people that get to him? Or only the Northern Irish. Our accent's not amenable like the Southern brogue, rich as Guinness. It's uncompromising, so I'm told. Aggressive. Then there's two of us in it – himself and me. And he's Welsh. I can tell. I've lived here long enough to be able to hear the markers in his accent. His Welshness is well-hidden – years of golfing and aspiration – but we're non-English, the two of us. Like it or not.

I wait. It's late July and a window is open. I'm used to waiting. I've been all over this hospital. I'm a 'thick-filer'. I overheard that. Not good. They think you're a fantasist, inventing symptoms, lying. But I never lie to them. What'd be the point of that? Not in my interests to hide the truth. Still, I've been sent to psychiatrists for 'failure to collaborate' because if the doctors can't cure me, clearly it's my fault. But I always *have* collaborated, had the injections, gone to the psychotherapy. I'm used to them looking at me, puzzled, irritated that I don't match their identikit. I look so normal.

Only once have I peeked at my file. 'This obviously highly intelligent young woman...' one entry in the opening pages began but someone grabbed it from me before I could read more, and such a glare I got, like I'd been nosing in someone else's life! What was that complimentary phrase a code for, I wonder. 'This awkward customer'? I've been told I have this or that, then had the diagnosis rescinded. I've been told to get a wheelchair, then not to get one. They've even told my family that I am choosing to be ill — there's no other explanation for my pain. And my nearest and dearest nod!

I am certainly used to waiting. Today's expert I have never seen before. He's not the first of his specialism to have had the pleasure of examining me but my G.P. doesn't know anything about him and that is precisely why he's sent me here. Is the G.P. embarrassed to be linked to me?

This consultant looked at me severely as he questioned me, like I was a criminal who'd dart off with something valuable if he didn't keep me in his sights. When he lowered his eyes, casually, I knew something was coming and... bam! up he came with a question that broke the mould, a question I'd never been asked before. And I lied. I told him one, single lie. He knew. He half-shut one eye and quizzed me with it but he didn't ask again. He smirked. He looked me up and down, meaning, "If a patient won't help herself...?"

Shall I tell him? When he comes back, shall I confess?

Shall I tell him how we had travelled a long way? I was eight. A city child. A hundred miles westwards was an expedition in nineteen-sixty-five and more so since my father could never afford a decent car and went from one banger to the next. We arrived (without breaking down) in a village that was one long, broad street. It reminded me of the cowboy films on tv where 'town' was the wide space between rows of shops that looked like houses, and houses fronted right onto the pavement, with a hotel, a bar and a smithy in the mix. Here, just as in the Westerns, lots of windows looked into the street, where the 'show-down' would happen, the drama in the empty road. But this place was staid. I couldn't imagine an act of public violence. "Nothing to see here, stranger."

The approach to the village had a huge church and an old-fashioned stone schoolhouse on one side; on the other a massive archway with elaborate gates opening onto an avenue which disappeared among trees. Daddy mentioned a double-barrelled name as we passed it. A Duke of Something. "The whole place grew up to serve them."

"Is that…?" Mammy murmured, pointing discreetly at the church.

Daddy nodded.

I knew it was a Protestant church because it was plainer, older and grander than any of ours. So it was something to do with religion they were keeping from me.

Daddy was excited but anxious. I knew what it was like to be unsure of the welcome you'd get. My friends in our Belfast street sometimes kept me out of certain 'special' games, 'because you're a Catholic'. They weren't nasty about it but clearly there was something obvious to them but hidden from me. Some fundamental difference separated me. I had no one to ask because we were the only Catholics in the street. I'd heard my father mention some Protestant cousins but, till this trip, I had never met any. I lived a Catholic life in a Protestant part of the city. I couldn't link those invisible relatives to my daily experience and since no one around me ever saw them, they counted for nothing, as credentials, where it really mattered, such as getting into those games. Yet, though I never told anyone, for me, even to know of them was a door into some possible belonging at some unimaginable point.

We went to what Daddy remembered as 'the family shop'. It was a butcher's now. The butcher was easy-going and waved us through, past the chops and hanging joints of meat and the white tiles, through the tang of blood, to a room behind, where all was shadowy. We stood in a back parlour. There was a high slate mantelpiece over a black range. "I never bothered with all that back there," the butcher called in after us. Indeed, he hadn't touched it at all. The lace curtains over the single window were yellow with dust. Ornaments and family bits and pieces and the cushions on the two armchairs sat where they had been left. Two calendars on the wall seemed to me particularly abandoned. No one had been interested enough to turn their pages as the months passed, and then the years. These things left behind; these little things more permanent than the individuals, continuing to exist regardless. "Go on out if you want to," the butcher shouted. "It's not locked."

We went through the scullery. Beyond the back door was a surprisingly big and bright yard, full of sunshine. There was a waist-high ring of brick in the centre; a low, open-fronted building to the right and a high gable wall glinting down at us. A man's name – my father's name – was painted high on it. *Blacksmith and Saddler.* "Your grandfather?" my mother asked him.

"Yes. And my father and uncle worked here too."

So it was a forge. These men I'd never met became suddenly more real. Their world flared, briefly, in sparks, and clinks, and hooves on the cobbles. That was my surname, up there. I had a connection with this place.

As we passed back through the parlour I was sorry to leave all the dusty things behind with no one to love them.

We went to another house. The woman who lived there frightened me. She was bent in two, like a witch in a fairy tale. Daddy's cousin, Sarah. Her fingers were bony and twisted. I tried not to show that I didn't like it when she grabbed my hand and looked eagerly up into my face. She had to look up – her head was bent so far downwards. What had she been looking for? "Oh, she's like you. She's like you, James," she said to him, pleased. "One of us, I'd say." She had big, beautiful eyes. The eyes of a princess. The body of a crone. I was sent out to the back almost at once, to get me out of the way while the grown-ups talked about something.

There was not much to see there but as an only child I was used to amusing myself. I found an interesting gutter running across the yard. It was made of units of smooth, black, stone-like something. I thought of those varnished wooden building blocks that richer children had – cubes, pyramids – and there were always just a few bridge-shaped pieces. Yes, the units were like those little bridges. I imagined someone building a tower of these black bridge-blocks and wondering what to do with it. Brainwave! Lay the tower on its back and you've got a channel. How nicely the pieces all fitted together, with no gaps. I thought of rain flowing off the roof, down a pipe and then along this open route. How clever to have made a single smooth thing from so many separate pieces, the joints laid athwart the flow of water.

But someone was crying in the house. I crept to the door. A man was shouting. I peeped in. A man was standing over the little woman. For a moment, I thought I knew him then I realised it was only that he had his face all twisted up, with his head on one side, pointing at Sarah just like the bully in the playground when he corners someone. Something heavy was in his other hand. "Think you can do what I have to?" he snarled. "Lady Muck! To keep *you*, rain or shine. Try this for size!" Suddenly he swung a big, bulging canvas bag towards her and dropped the wide leather strap over her bent back. She staggered under its weight and whimpered. "Complaining *now*!" he mocked.

He pushed her towards the back of the house with one hand and with the other pointed warningly at Daddy who had moved towards her. Sarah's eyes were wide and full of tears. The man said, slowly and triumphantly, "Man and wife. Man. And. Wife." From behind him Sarah shook her head at my parents, scared. Daddy stepped back. The man bent to the floor and picked up two letters and a postman's cap. "Here!" he called to Sarah, "You dropped these." He tossed them at her. He crushed the cap down on her head. "On your way! Folks are waiting." The bag was overflowing with letters. He looked at my parents with a smile I recognised: a you-can't-touch-me smile; a tell-on-me-and-she-gets-it smile.

Daddy muttered, "The child." and I darted to the farthest end of the yard, knowing I wasn't supposed to have seen any of this. Mammy waved me towards her, grabbing my hand very tightly as soon as I was within reach. She pulled me through the room and out to the street where, ahead of us, Daddy was striding towards the car. Mammy shoved sixpence into my hand and pushed me towards a sweet shop opposite.

When I'd secured the unexpected treat of an ice cream I lingered in the shop so I could watch them through its window. My daddy thumped the car with his closed fist. My mammy was gnawing her thumb and looking anxiously back at that house. What would they do? How did you rescue a witch? The witch holds people captive; the witch makes the prince carry out terrible tasks to set the princess free. If the witch was the princess…?

Was she really going to have to hump those letters from door to door while the people looked on and did nothing?

I knew better than to ask any questions straight away. After many miles, when they thought I was asleep in the back seat, my parents talked. Daddy remembered her as a lovely young girl.

Fond of the fashion. Took over the Post Office when her mother died. Well set up. Centre of everything, the Post Office.

Who is he? my mother asked.

A bye-blow. A chancer. Born the wrong side of the blanket but, bold as you like, flaunted the same name as His Grace, the Duke. Married Sarah for the Post Office − expecting an easy life. Yes, she had been lovely.

So she wasn't always − like that?

No. It came on after her marriage. Some say she was dropped as a baby....

Mammy snorted at that.

As they went on I thought of her being dropped. It's what people used to say, isn't it? Explanation for anything that goes wrong. An accident. Or a wicked fairy. Someone who wished the child ill, who wished someone else could bear the burden of ugliness, know what it's like to be embarrassment, to not get your due.

Here he is back again, Dr. Pepper. "Stand!" he orders, and he pronounces a diagnosis. I grasp 'spinal fusion' and 'genetic marker' and 'incurable'. He thrusts a leaflet at me. "It's all in there." He'll write to my G.P. I am dismissed, with contempt. He knows I lied. He'd asked if anyone in the family was very bent and I said, 'No.' Failure to collaborate.

I had to lie. Sarah had suddenly looked up at me, taking my hand. I hadn't wanted to expose her to that contemptuous man. I didn't want it to be her fault.

I understood what the consultant was trying to get at − hadn't I seen it in that yard? − the separate parts jointed together into a whole; the spinal vertebrae fused into a smooth column; no gaps and so no movement. The body bends like a palm tree, the head a heavy fruit on the rigid stalk of the neck. A genetic flaw.

Something triggers a disproportionate reaction in the bones – food poisoning; an infection. Bad luck. Bad fairy.

So, Sarah is what's ahead of me. At this stage I'm still upright but the prognosis is rigidity, pain and a bent back. But I feel relieved – relieved not to be mad. It's the fault of the genes, those little, persistent things, outlasting the individual lives, busy about their work inside the family.

My long-widowed mother will link me and Sarah as soon as I tell her about the condition, whether or not the science supports that. She'll be appalled at the thought of the deformity predicted for me but having someone she can think of it as being 'handed-down from' will console her. She likes to have a story to fit things into.

And I know the end of Sarah's story. All those years earlier, my parents had written to the local vicar, asking him to do something about the appalling relationship. He'd replied that he couldn't interfere. My parents had no further leverage on 'the other side'.

A couple of years ago my mother asked me to go back. Even after forty years she was uneasy about Sarah. I found a local historian who was glad someone, anyone, from the family was asking about the past. He brought us to the Protestant churchyard. Some sort of maintenance upheaval had seen many grave markers removed, he told us, indignantly. Without him, I'd never have found the grave.

The blacksmith – my father's uncle – and the post-mistress – my father's aunt, are in there. They are Sarah's parents and she's beside them, with the chancer. He had his good moments, the local man insisted. A cypress, an actual cypress – aristocratic, classical, a gently swaying tongue of bottle-green flame – a cypress grows out of the grave.

As I walk away from the consultant, I think of their bones amongst the roots. I think of my bones. I think of my Protestant grandfather, uncle to Sarah, who left his brother at the forge and married 'the Catholic', against all reason; who lived amongst 'his own' in defiance of gain-saying and left me an outlier in their midst: exposed, attentive and watchful; interested in bridges; in collaboration – and survival.

SAINT

They were seated around an 'O' of parquet flooring in a large, sunny room. These theatre people liked circles, Alicia thought. "We're all in this together," Madge kept asserting as she got them to re-group the chairs, but somehow the new shape didn't make them equal to him, to Theo Kane. They should really have been put into a triangle, Alicia considered silently, because he was at the apex of this circle (whether a circle could have one or not) because people leaned in his direction, sought his unspoken approval. He was their point of reference. Alicia examined him covertly. He said almost nothing yet the course of the discussion was directed by him. She could see that he only had to signal assent, boredom or disapproval to effect a change.

At the start of the session she hadn't known who he was but he had instantly stood out among the adults. His clothes, his physique, his good looks and his air of waiting for the eddying people to settle around him marked him out as special, polished, coming from another world. Madge – Theo's assistant, who'd got her in – steered them through the practicalities with breezy statements. They were in this together, she repeated: professionals and amateurs. They owned the production jointly. That was what community theatre was all about. Was it really, Alicia wondered, because the decisions they reached were never not his.

She was pleased with herself for spotting this. She despised herself for wishing he could know she had. So she said nothing, but, in her own internal theatre, she quashed and outshone the others' remarks. By the time the session ended, she felt worn out, and irritated with him for being able to affect her like this. He just had to sit there, being beautiful and.... Could a man be beautiful? She was seventeen and she wasn't interested in old men. Theo was... could be... nearly in his forties. He looked like no one she'd ever met − not actually been in the same room as them. He was so... clean! He was the director. She supposed she'd have to get used to men like him now she was to be an actress. She had, she knew, decided late in life. Some of her friends had been in theatre groups since they were tots. No use in worrying about it.

As people pushed back chairs, talked of lunch, detained each other for 'a word', she watched him continue to sit, one leg crossed over the other, lounging back in the uncomfortable institutional chair, his gaze on the floor as he was spoken to by the large, florid, noisy man seated on his right. Many people had wanted to speak to him but this man had caught him.

Theo Kane, the centre of their universe, wore a sweater of fine wool, of the palest pink, draped around his shoulders with its arms flopped into his lap, across his white shirt. He stood, knotting the sleeves at his breast bone. He was blond and lightly tanned. He seemed to belong to a different species to the man who continued to jab the air to emphasise his points.

As this man lumbered to his feet, Alicia saw the instant when Theo repressed a spasm of distaste for him. The man, oblivious, detained him with further emphases. She would never be so crass, she thought, that she'd fail to see when it was time to stop. She walked past them and, as she did so, Theo suddenly addressed her, "You didn't say anything."

She turned. The man, arrested in mid-flow, his hand on Kane's arm, gawped at her. For a moment, all three stood in a silent tableau till the man removed his hand and took a step, resentfully, backwards.

"Please excuse me," Theo said to him, looking him straight in the eye.

The man, catching the intensity more than the meaning, nodded and waved him away, glowing with satisfaction at being able to serve his hero.

Alicia was swept towards the door somehow, though not touched, and outside, Theo smiled at her. "Thank God there's someone with nothing to say!" he whispered. He moved on, then turned back. He inspected her intently. "Of course," he added, "those are the ones one has to watch most carefully." He left.

She was flattered and at the same time didn't like feeling so affected. She thrust her chin in the air and headed in the opposite direction.

Three months later she walked into his bedroom, one of several bedrooms in his London flat. She stopped after a few steps, waiting for the door to close behind her. She had never been in a room like this. She couldn't move till she had taken it in. Everything was white. Every thing. It made her dizzy to consider the implications. Someone had chosen each item, rejecting this, selecting that, until the perfect assemblage of white had been achieved. No compromise. No 'But it's a perfectly good bed... lamp... pair of curtains.'

If it didn't fit the scheme, it wasn't good enough, presumably. Not good enough for the person who slept here. There was money here, was there? It would take a lot of money to have enough to spend satisfying this particular desire, for a white bedroom. For a white spare bedroom!

She touched the white bedspread. It was heavily ridged, with white fringes which arranged themselves gracefully on the white carpet. Colourless muslin blinds blanched the summer evening light which filled the room with a texture of its own.

How could she sleep in such whiteness? But there were white, robustly lined ceiling-to-floor drapes framing the pretty Edwardian sash windows. They thought of everything, he and his wife.

His wife seemed nice though she fluttered between the rooms of the flat a little anxiously, Alicia thought, wanting Alicia to feel at home. Not likely! The flat was... quality. Everything was what her mother would call 'good'. There was an older woman there too. Ancient. She had a voice which sounded like it was giving orders, even when it wasn't. She had a silly name: Pippa.

Pippa sounded like a little girl's name. Theo paid plenty of attention to *her*. She had very brown skin as though she'd lived under a fierce sun for years and her face was as lined as those channels in dried-up river beds you see in photos of disasters. She was lean. Old people were usually white and bulgy. On Pippa's brown, bony fingers were three rings with loads of diamonds, and one giant one. You'd think an old, old person like that would give up on rings and stuff. Start giving it away.

They had had 'drinks' together. Alicia had insisted on lemonade. "Quite right," said ancient Pippa. Alicia had felt out of her depth in the conversation with its references to people she didn't know and theatre stuff, though it was exciting too, to think this was all to be learnt.

Theo's wife had slightly protruding eyes. Had they got that way through her constant effort of paying attention to him? Because she never took her eyes off him. She was a little breathless with the effort. Alicia noticed there were fine hairs on Theo's forearms which matched the colour of the whiskey in his cut-glass tumbler. 'Cut-glass'. That's what Pippa's accent was called. Why? Because there was an edge to it, clipped, hard, like a laser? Did a laser cut glass? Another thing she didn't know.

Pippa contradicted and challenged Theo freely and Alicia thought he sulked a bit in return. Then Pippa suddenly leant forwards towards him and said, with quite a different tone, "But you, darling, you're above all that. You deserve better – the best."

He seemed to gulp this down and then he leant towards her – Alicia thought he was going to kiss her – but nothing happened. They just sat there, sort of nose-to-nose. His wife stood up suddenly and said a few vague words which didn't even make a sentence. Her gaze darted jerkily around the room. Alicia thought of a bird that had been trapped in her kitchen once. It too had shot from side to side. Perhaps his wife was simply very short-sighted. Then the wife was looking at her and Alicia said she'd like to go to bed. Of course, of course, replied the wife. Early start. Leeds was quite a drive.

Alicia inserted herself into the white bed like a letter sliding into an envelope. When she woke the next morning, she was pleased to see it looked undisturbed, as though no one had been in it.

"Yes, I've got her the paper, darling. I remembered, I remembered. And the cranberry juice. She's feeling a little fragile." Theo's wife's voice passed down the corridor outside the bedroom, sounding fragile itself. A door was opened at a distance and her voice suddenly went bright in greeting, "Here we are, Pippa!"

Getting into Theo's car a little later, Alicia let his wife close the door behind her because its scarlet bodywork was so shiny she didn't want to leave finger-marks. She noticed Theo glancing at himself in the mirror even before the car moved. He was taking her to Leeds himself because she'd had to tell Madge she couldn't afford the fare to the audition. Madge had told her she just had to get herself to London by bus. And the rest would be taken care of.

"He must want you," Mam had murmured wonderingly.

"As 'Saint Catherine's Sister'," Alicia explained.

"Ugly Sister!" her brother quipped.

"Married, is he?" Mam asked. Then a round of phone calls and Mam even insisting on speaking to his wife "in person please". "You wait!" Mam had said to Alicia. "You wait and see what men can't be bothered with!" Which wasn't much of a vote of confidence, was it? Not much of a compliment.

It was a long way to Leeds. After a while he asked her to turn off her mobile because her friends kept texting and calling. The car sped and hummed. She decided to ask him about the film. "Haven't you seen the script?" he asked. She explained it hadn't arrived. He told her the story.

"Well," she said, in response, "I don't get why anyone would do that."

"What?"

"Kill themselves just because they got dumped."

He looked sharply at her. "He loved her."

"Yes."

"And she left him."

"So?"

"'So'?" he repeated indignantly.

"So what? He didn't have to *die.*"

"Haven't you ever been in love?"

"Not so's to make me want to kill myself!" She could tell he didn't like this reply.

He drove on for some time without speaking. She looked at the passing scenery.

"You're a pragmatist, then," he observed suddenly.

"I don't know what that means."

"You go for what works. You don't have dreams, dreams you want to pursue no matter what."

"I have dreams!" She turned towards him. He kept his eyes on the road. Oh, very handy, she thought, annoyed. He wore a blue denim shirt, open at the throat. Its cuffs were turned back on his forearms and these were tensed as he gripped the wheel. What was the big deal? "But you've got to live, too," she insisted.

"Living's what matters, is it?" he retorted.

"Yes!"

"Without dreams? Without ideals? Say your ideal woman rejects you... can't you imagine not wanting to live?"

"Nobody should be that important."

He looked at her at once. "Goodbye Romeo and Juliet. Goodbye Antony and Cleopatra, Othello...."

"Yeah!" she shrugged. "Goodbye! You can't *live* like that. You have to make an effort."

"But the effort can be too much!" he insisted, switching his gaze back to the road.

"Well, people should try harder!"

"You think they *don't* try?"

She sniffed.

"You have no idea!" he said bitterly.

I do, she thought. Mam. Dad.

Her silence incensed him. "Catherine sends her lover away when she turns to God. He kills himself, alone."

"Stupid him."

"He *loved* her!"

"She had a better offer." Alicia muttered, "Get over it."

"What? What did you say? You think some insubstantial pie in the sky, some 'relationship' with God is better than a real living, breathing human being?" She didn't answer. "She refused to see him," he went on. "She stayed in the house for days rather than meet him. She never answered his letters."

"Of course not! It's the kindest thing to do."

"Speaking from experience?"

No way was she going there. It wasn't a competition. She heard him make a little contemptuous noise, then say, "It's people who matter. People." He glanced in the driving-mirror and gave a nod to his reflection. "Yes. She was safe in her virtue, I suppose, wasn't she? She was doing nothing wrong. Oh, no." He glanced through the side window for a moment but she knew he was not seeing what was outside. He was remembering something and, sure enough, he spoke slowly and emphatically. "I have held people all night in my arms. All night. That's what they need. Not to be alone." He shook his head, his face beautiful in profile. "Nobody should be left alone."

Alicia saw him, with his arms, in blue denim, around a vague figure who huddled desperately in their embrace. Theo the refuge, all night long. And the dawn was whitening the darkness and then.... Theo wouldn't be there. What then? What about us, she found herself thinking. Yeah. What about us, she demanded with increasing fierceness: the ordinary ones, the plain ones, the red-faced, awkward, lumpy ones. In the broad light of day what would we do then? He'd be safe in his virtue. Theo the saviour. Our final crumbling merely postponed. And when we did hit the dust, up it would rise like perfume. Snuffing us up, he'd be.

Not me, she resolved. She would get this part and be so good he'd want her again. She was a professional. His equal. She would be sitting in that circle on equal terms, saying, 'No, thank you' to the handsome man − if she felt like it. Like Catherine. She made sure not to smile, pressing her lips into a hard line, even though this insight made her heart leap and − Good, she approved herself. Good. You can do it.

COASTEERING

'Dinnae ower-think it!' Alec urged, and then repeated himself. I chose not to explain that what I was doing was savouring the moment: a woman in her element, teetering on a needle-point of rock thrust up among a jumble of black basalt that out-faced the heaving sea around us. Below me the cold-coloured water never broke into foam. It flexed and stretched and contracted. It pulled itself down between facing outcrops as though determined to vanish through a sink-hole then surged up gleefully, flicking its tail. It was in no hurry and neither was I but the evening light was losing colour and that blanching was a sure sign of fading day. No instructor would want to be out here in the dark.

I loosened the cuffs of the waterproof jacket that added a layer to the battered old wetsuit he'd provided. Seawater gushed out past my wrists. I poised myself, leapt – an un-timeable gap – and was smothered in crashing bubbles and noise and resistance, then broke upwards into air and the push and pull of the sea. This was what I'd wanted, to be out beyond the little beaches and rock-strewn shores; to be out of my depth but safe; to be gripped by the sea's power but not at its mercy. I respect the sea. I fear it.

As I relished the swirl of the water around me, I thought of how often I'd stood on dry sand or crunchy pebbles or in the shallows, constrained to watching waves rushing against far-off stretches of rock. This is a coastline where spectacularly large, cliff-lined bays are skirted with clusters of tiny inlets hardly more than finger-holds for the sea. From these little beaches, cobs of dark volcanic rock jut out, pitted like black honeycomb but displaying too the swerving symmetry of lava waves frozen in their tracks millennia ago. In one particular little nook the water just beyond my depth had always looked as though it had a sandy floor and perhaps the swell was manageable there but it was hard to tell. I never took the risk.

This summer – the first without children or young grown-ups – I'd realised I could venture further. I could go coasteering. Someone expert could ensure I didn't come a cropper out there. Out at sea.

Unlike those massive blue stretches of the far south, our northern Irish sea has no steady colour. It takes its hue from the coming and going of the sun as it parts clouds – to raise – from the dun acres of water far below, shining fields of vivid jade wrapped in the darkest bottle-green. Seen from cliff-tops, these colours display themselves as vast sheets of luminous intensity. One of the attractions of coasteering was that, close-up, they would tilt and rock beneath me like stained glass panels miraculously made flexible. Most wonderful of all, they could be entered. I could be part of those glowing colour-pools. And I had done it. Even if today that brilliance was fitful and we had started later than we meant to.

Alec shouted something, pointing westward. Like me, he was in his fifties. He was portly and easy-going. I felt a pleasant confidence in him, perhaps because he wasn't a typical coasteering pro. No sprightly young athlete, he was a dogged local man. The two of us had had three outings together. I enjoyed doing what he told me: swim, clamber, jump, crawl. It was a great way to let go of time.

He was indicating now a huge pile of rock stretching further out to sea than anything we'd come on so far. We were separated from it by a broad stretch of open water. In we plunged. Though I seemed to make hardly any progress I relaxed into the rhythmic efforts which would eventually get me to our goal. I stopped now and then to look up at the pale sky; to notice water, brownish and yet transparent; both lucid and richly supportive. It was, bizarrely, like swimming in scentless Guinness.

Anyone will tell you that getting out of the water is more of a challenge than getting in. With one hand I clung at last to a rock – its coating of tiny shells abrasive as a cheese grater – while the sea tugged my body in the opposite direction, straining my arm-socket almost past endurance; but I knew that if I waited calmly the returning surge would lift me forward so I could get a purchase, and hoist myself out. And, with that, I was raised by a wave and deposited on a limpet-covered ledge.

Alec called to me, pointing towards the horizon. "D'ye see oot thair? Whut's oot thonner? Icelan mebbe? Naethin but watther." I made my way to him and we gazed across the vast expanse. "A year bak," he said quietly, "A came here i'tha dairk. Aye. Mad, it waes. An thaim Northren Lichts – can ye picthur it? – big green curtins ower ma heid. Sae far aff." I watched him wonder at the memory and smiled to think I'd been wrong about night-time jaunts. "We shud be goin in," he went on, "but, 'less ye be agin it, we cud take a wee dannther roon tae tha en. It'll be a while or iver ye get oot this lenth agane."

We headed towards the seaward edge of the outcrop. He showed me pools fringed with delicate weed and studded with sea anemones, their colours muted and bluish in the failing light. We manoeuvred around the base of the stack, hanging on by fingers and toes. We passed strange deep holes going a few metres horizontally back into the rock. They echoed our shouts. But I couldn't follow him all the way to the ocean face. It was beyond me.

"Go you on," he said, "tae tha nixt wee bay. Let yersel in an A'll be wi' ye afore lang."

I enjoyed the chance to watch the sea. It was force made visible by its effects as it pushed broad straps of kelp, fastened to the rocks below the waterline, now shoreward, now seaward, and sent spurts of tide-water steadily making ground over the lowest slabs. If you think too much about it – about how puny you are in a power-filled universe – you'd never do anything. Coasteering is one of those undertakings – like childbirth – in which the only momentum is forward. There's no opting out once you're in.

I made my way over a ridge and edged down the other side. Only as I was about to enter the water did I look landward and recognise, with a shock, exactly where I found myself: the nondescript little cove was that particular one from which I had so often looked out, wishing I could get further.

Nobody knew the significance of this place to me. It was where I used to come to cry – or weep, in fact, for only weeping has that given-way-to quality as though something is weeping you. Weeping: for what could not be had, not be risked; for what must be shouldered, not shirked.

On holiday here, I used to leave the house early before children or husband stirred and trudge to this beach because it offered shelter from wind and curiosity. It was a natural place to stop and take stock of the scenery, or the weather. A woman huddled against that rock would not be remarkable to a rare passer-by. There had to be some place where I could lower my guard and give way. I knew weeping achieved nothing except some temporary release. It solved no problem but when it was over I could re-set my will and labour to be un-laboured.

Now I wondered, when I had leant against that rock and wept, was I acknowledging that I was up against something stronger than myself? I stared at the sea's unending shuffle forward and retreat, recalling how it felt to be shoved onward by it and sucked back. No. I hadn't been in the grip of a force outside myself. It was something within me. I had been buffeted by some current in myself deeper than I was used to negotiating.

I seemed to see, across the boulder-strewn foreshore, a small figure on that rapidly darkening beach. How extraordinary that my memories were, to her, the life she still had to face. She had looked into the unknowable – which I now knew. To see her from here was to live again her sapping, persistent feeling of being inadequate; of not having what was required; of living at my limit and it still not being enough. To inflict pain deliberately is one thing; to be the cause of pain despite my best efforts had been, for me, a horrific double torture; as though a tyrant had arranged my tormented existence to be the instrument of torment to someone beloved. Who wouldn't, then, prefer to vanish? Except the appalling mechanism's calibration would produce in that case an even more dreadful pain: an inadequate wife but his only wife; the children's only mother; the only, disappointing, daughter-in-law; hollow; resourceless. That had been me.

Yet, here I was, out in the bay, at last able to look back from that point I'd wanted to reach. The family was intact, in their various locations; some in their graves.

I thought of my mother, in extreme old age, her bright faculties striving against her collapsing body. In the last conversation I ever had with her, days before her death, she'd repeated the words, 'lamb' and 'jam'. I'd probably been the only person in the world who could have understood what she was remembering and trying to share. It was Lamb's jam factory, where more than eighty years earlier, many of her school-mates were sent to work. They all died of TB, fostered by the damp, warm conditions. Those girls, barely into their teens, had returned to her. Maybe she had been looking back over her life, from its furthest reach, telling over again the immense effects of her mother's refusal to send her among the boiling fruit and bottling jars, whatever help the money would have been.

I gave my mother, that day, the words she couldn't supply and saw her glad to have that experience, that loss, surviving in someone else's mind. We all want to live. One day, further on, I might be like her, looking back to this very moment from an edge I couldn't, at this point, imagine.

I was chilled from standing. I felt a hand on my shoulder and tears on my face. Alec was inspecting me with concern. "The salt gets in my eyes," I said.

"Aye, it daes that," he agreed. There was a pause. "Afore we gae bak A jest want tae remine ye o' tha basics." I nodded, not looking at him. "Credit tha watther tae houl ye up an mine yer braithe."

I turned, surprised.

"Aff ye wurnae tae draw braithe, whut hope wud thair be? An credit tha watther or ye'll wear yersel oot thrishin an thrashin."

I gazed at him. Was that it? Breathe. Believe.

"Are we fur tha shore?" he asked briskly.

I nodded. But as I lowered myself towards the water I was, again, that woman on the beach, hearing an inner voice: *You can love more than this;* panicked at such a demand but then attentive; heeding it as an extravagant invitation, not sadism. What more could I do? Simply accept that what I could do was likely to fall short. When all is expended some other force has to step forward – or not. If the time to drown has come, so be it. If the tide buoys you up, good. Do your part, not more.

"Onlie lukin bak dae ye see hoo far ye hae come," Alec said.

"We'r oot this three oors."

"Will you bring me here to see the Northern Lights?" I asked suddenly.

"Ye'd venture that?" He laughed, pleased. "Aye, A wull. A wull surely."

SALTEM

He found the bookshop bewildering. There was order but only just. It had the air of a place where books come to expire and in the warm weather it was full of a dry heat. Among the shelves and stacks there was a single completely tidy element, a very tall, glass-fronted bookcase, kept locked, and on top of this were lined up other 'choice' volumes too large to fit inside.

He had come in with her. Why not? Anyone can browse. They got on well, which surprised him − no, what surprised him was how much he talked in her company. He didn't usually say much. He was a painter. He didn't want to speak as well!

Familiar irritation rose in him. People wanted stuff, wanted you to say things and then they wanted commitments and under-takings. He shivered. He never even named his works. Numbered them, yes. They were enough in themselves. What was the point in having a reputation if you couldn't get your own way?

She was out of sight beyond some shelves. He looked around. A tatty place, buffed and scuffed yet ticking quietly with potential. One might find a gem here. He felt content again. Titles every-where here, of course. *The Cities of Umbria,* its spine sturdily embossed with stylised lilies. Edwardian. Yes, published 1905. The facing page carried the dedication, '*To Alice*' and a line below in Latin which meant nothing to him. The date of dedication too, '*May 21, 1904*'. More than a century ago.

The book was illustrated with watercolour plates which were

too smudgily indistinct for his taste and the prose was over-wrought. Of a town called Todi (near Perugia, apparently – he didn't know it),

"Ah! It is not happy, that great modern world from which I have fled. And why? Has it not driven Beauty away to such eagle-nests as this? And it is here indeed, we find her in tears, but free upon the mountains. Not chained in the galleries of the cities of the people, where even the most brutal and the most base may gaze upon her and defile her with their thoughts...."

Steady on! Was his own work ever defiled by the thoughts of '*the most base*'? But why consider other people's thoughts? He didn't care much about who was going to look at his work when he was actually making. It was him and that shape he was changing – square, rectangle.

'*Beauty....*' with a capital 'B', eh? No doubt personified, seen as a languid, Grecian-profiled damsel in voluminous draperies, weeping (but never less than picturesque). As for the brutal and the base! He felt aggressive, hackles up, ready to defend his space, his square. Maybe he did care about other people's thoughts.

He flicked ahead in the book. '*She is a dead city that I have loved*'. Morbid. Where was the author writing about now? Urbino. Well, mate, Urbino was thriving these days. World Heritage Site. "Stuff you," he murmured.

"Disagreement?" she said, smiling at him.

"I...." Disconcerted, he aimed for another topic. "What does this mean?" he asked, showing her the Latin phrase.

'*In hoc saltem libro inveniam faciem tuam*', she read. '*Saltem*' – a word I don't know. Hang on. Bound to be a Latin diction-ary...." She vanished. Her voice reached him, '*At least*'. OK," she said, reappearing. Scrutinising the line, she translated, '*At least in this book I will come upon – find – your face*'.

A vanished face. A lost face. Melancholy silenced them. He felt chastened. Poor bloke. He forgave him the purple prose. It was an effort but....

"Do you think Alice was dead?" she asked quietly.

"Do people dedicate books to the dead?" He replaced the book, adding, "Kind of thing this guy would do."

"Fidelity-Beyond-The-Grave?" she suggested.

"Clingy," he sniffed, with distaste.

She turned away to hide a smile, thinking of his well-known reluctance to join or belong to anything, a position maintained for two decades at least; even rumoured to take offence at offers to buy his work; how he never invited anyone to his home and preferred brief meetings in public places. She had been surprised when, their tea-shop interview concluded, he had followed her into the bookshop.

Since their first appointment, she had taken her cue from him. She had arrived at a venue unfamiliar to her and spotted him waiting. Covertly, he was stretching his right hand, clenching and opening it. He looked into his palm, splaying the fingers and contracting them. He was assessing its flexibility. His face was shadowed with anxiety.

Feeling she had witnessed a vulnerability which was private, she had turned and left the building. Re-entering a few moments later, as though having just arrived, she had deliberately greeted him while still at some distance. The face he turned to her was composed. She admitted to herself that she treated him with particular gentleness from that point.

She looked at him now as he peered in through the glass of the locked case. Funny, she thought, how making things inaccessible increased their appeal. Could be any old rubbish in there, really. She looked higher and saw an intriguing title in the row on the top. She cast around for something to stand on.

"Let me," he offered. "That one, is it?"

He reached up but the books were so jammed together he couldn't get a purchase on the volume. It was also more of a stretch than he'd expected. He planted his weight on the ball of his left foot so the whole right side of his body could push up as far as possible. She stepped back to give him more room. He tried again. She looked on.

His index finger was pointing up, pressed to the spine of the book. Its finger-tip, she realised gradually, was the high point of a line, that dropped − with a blip over the delicate nub of his wrist-bone − down along the inner side of his forearm into the elbow's hollow (where the rolled-up shirt-sleeve fell back on un-sunned skin), falling to, and over, the splayed shoulder-hinge, down his torso into the shallow contour of his waist where it crested the hoisted hip before plunging the length of the leg to the foot at full stretch, the toes' fractional contact with the floor earthing the line at last.

It was a beautiful line, like a dancer's captured in a photograph; a line born from effort yet languid to see. She stored the sight of it and was aware of wanting to run the palm of her hand along the line, to feel it.

As he tried to ease the book out from under its bottom edge he wondered suddenly, "Is she watching me?" He became intensely conscious of his body, of its being on full, prolonged display, like an artist's model. Yeah! Like an artist's model depicting some bloody Edwardian ideal: *Ad Astra!* or *Excelsior! Onward and Upward!* − their cherished pastiches of the Classics and the play-ing-field. Then he found, amongst the irritation, he didn't mind the thought of her gaze travelling over him. In fact, he realized with astonishment, he would be disappointed if it wasn't. With a last effort, he dislodged the book, grabbed it and gave it to her.

She took it and examined it. He felt slightly light-headed, knocked off-centre. He stared at a shelf to compose himself. What on earth was he feeling? Hope, he thought − and, yes, he would indeed personify like a good Edwardian − Hope lifts her noble, Grecian head, sensing some shift on the horizon. He felt suddenly moved, then his head dropped: Despair. The thickets to breach and the tortuous wrangles and accommodations and explanations and sheer *time…* and anyway, *look at me*! His deficiencies mocked him.

She was speaking to him. "I'm glad to have seen that. Thanks. I have to go." She held out her hand.

Unready, he fumbled somehow so that she ended up grasping, not his hand, but his bare forearm. He felt her finger-tip brush near the pulse in the crook of his arm as she moved her hand away. She disappeared.

A vanished face. A lost face. No! His body was humming with connection, translating her into meaning. He wanted to deny it − nothing had been said − but he was already aware he was speculating, "At least… at least I could phone her." He looked up and saw her hesitate outside. She was looking into her hand as though reading something amazing.

RESISTANCE

Living in Thorndyke Avenue was like living in a chasm. Once you got in, there was only one way out. To Lily, an avenue (even in prosaic Belfast) was a straight, tree-lined approach to something, but Thorndyke Avenue was laid out in a shape like an office staple. By either one of the two short ends a ninety-degree turn led you between terraces of dark-red brick, eyeing each other across the overly narrow road, till you went down the second short arm onto the main road. This was fronted by a yet more massive terrace that stood back to back with Thorndyke Avenue.

The Avenue's houses were late Victorian, very plain, very tall and disproportionately thin. The sun found it hard to get down into this fissure and yet, Lily thought, it was at its worst on the hottest days of the year when the terraces flung heat back off each other as though tossing a hysterical relative from one unharbouring home to the next. Each house was separated from the pavement by a meagre, railed area. A Protestant church flanked one of the short ends.

The other end was dominated by an army barracks. Every day, to get home from her bus stop, Lily walked up the slight incline between two rows of identical houses built directly onto the pavements. They were high, flat-fronted and hard-faced, giving away nothing about the lives inside. Ahead, she looked up at the enormous, blank metal doors of the barracks. The foot patrols would emerge in two single files and she would walk between them, against a current of boots, berets, guns, and radio crackle, with the clang and boom of the gates echoing off the house-fronts. She would push through the pressure of the soldiers' eyes. How do you walk home constructively, Lily wondered, against the flow of so many gazes? They suspect. They assess. They dismiss – except when they choose to communicate: usually contempt; a racial contempt, mixed with the pleasure of revenge on the enemy through sexual disdain. How do you not treat them as they treat you?

Every day she braced herself for this encounter. She wouldn't avoid it by entering at the church end. It was her private battle, her struggle to do something good. If she looked away, kept her eyes down, that was cowardice. She would not engage in hostilities. She would not avoid the clash either. She returned the looks, as frankly as she could, despite her fear, her self-consciousness, and a scruple that she was being ridiculous. She would treat the soldiers as human beings. If they spoke, "Hello, Miss." "Nice day." She'd reply, "Hello." "Yes." She would do what good she could.

It was always a relief to get around the corner. The soldiers never came up the long stretch of the Avenue. The main road was their province and even more so the mesh of easily barricaded, bewilderingly similar Catholic streets on the far side of it. The Presbyterian church commanded a view into the heart of this battleground: row upon row of little houses filling the sloping land between the hills and the great sea lough which narrows into the port of Belfast. Thorndyke Avenue was above all that, a kind of hidden cleft. Yet more and more people who lived in it were Catholic. How did we get here, Lily wondered? What tide tossed us up so high?

One day she picked up a paper in the hall. It was something completely unprecedented, an invitation to a coffee morning. She had heard of coffee mornings! English people had them. English people on the television. Those English people were somehow different to the soldiers, who were also English. This coffee morning was an invitation to 'all our neighbours' from the Presbyterian church. Well, that explained it. English people and Protestants and coffee mornings went together. "Come and meet our youth team," the invitation read.

Lily pitied them. Did they not realise that most of their neighbours would never have been near a coffee morning; that they would find the idea both alien and laughable; a gap too wide to cross; an insult all the greater for having been given, probably, unconsciously? She was indignant. But at least they were trying. You shouldn't spurn advances. Meet them half-way. No harm. Some good.

On the Saturday morning, Lily knocked on the door of the manse. That's what a notice-board said it was, a manse. The date 1881 was carved over the door in huge numerals. Exactly a century ago. A youngish woman answered and immediately called over her shoulder, "James!" Then she muttered something that sounded like, "Sorry." and waved Lily towards a half-open door. Lily went in and eight or nine faces turned towards her in a sudden silence. They were all, like her, in their twenties. They looked, placed her, and turned to fussing with cups and milk.

She knew they were all Protestants: their clothes, more redolent of washing-powder; their hair more barbered or 'done'; their dexterity with the etiquette of teaspoon/saucer/home-baking more honed than any Catholics of their age. Yet they looked ill at ease. She realised suddenly that she was the only 'neighbour' there. No one else had come. Of course not, she thought sadly.

The young people stood in a tight formation, overly occupied with trivial exchanges. She sensed in them a kind of panic, like birds that register a predator at hand − a communal tremble and flutter. Drawing on her training with the soldiers, she kept her head up. She held a look here and there. She smiled. She gave them time. She spoke clearly, "Hello." It sounded like a challenge. "You're the youth team. I'm a neighbour." They looked almost ashamed for her. Did she not know her place, they visibly marvelled. They were the initiators. She should speak when spoken to.

Into the silence came a man in his thirties. He introduced himself as Pastor James Carleton and obliged some of the young people to shake hands with Lily. She and he were quickly marooned at one end of the room.

His parishioners, he told her, tiredly, were drifting away to safer areas, coming back to services fearfully and less often. "They just say they don't feel at home anymore." Lily could hear a baby fretting in a distant room as he explained awkwardly that he'd thought it time to do some outreach. He glanced across the empty space towards his young people, huddled together but chafing now, growing noisier. He sighed. "Everything around here's locked up, isn't it? Locked behind grills and wire. The pub across the road – sandbags outside. At night we can see right across the city: when the army moves in; when a mob gathers. I can spot them getting together stashes of petrol bombs. My wife's in bits. But you feel you have to do something. Not run away."

"It's the coffee," Lily offered. "Next time try tea so that...." The door opened sharply and his wife said in a tight voice, without appearing from behind it, "James!" He grimaced apologetically as he left. She set her cup down next to rows of unused china. "Goodbye. Lovely to meet you." The youth team mumbled in reply.

That night, Lily lay in bed and heard for hours the noises reaching her over the palisades of the double terrace: sirens, army vehicles whining past, the orchestrated clatter of a baton charge and broken waves of human voices, shrieking. She didn't bother looking out for she would see nothing. It was all happening in the main road. At six o' clock she got up. Things had quietened down. The radio told her that Bobby Sands's hunger-strike had ended with his death.

An hour later she walked around the corner by the church to wait for a lift to work outside Mrs McKee's. This morning something crunched underneath her feet – broken glass; a lot of it – odd, where there were no broken windows. This morning the main road was empty of traffic. There must be an army cordon somewhere. This morning the air smelt at once burnt and sickly. Last night's crowds had vanished.

She came out onto the main road and was confronted by the pole of a streetlight bent towards her by the weight of a milk float that was rammed into it at an odd angle. Right outside Mrs McKee's house. Milk crates must have slewed off the float when it crashed. It was their shards that carpeted the pavements. Several crates remained on its open-sided lorry-back, the silver bottle-tops winking in the May sunlight. The road glittered too and scraps of coloured paper moved gently along its surface in the breeze like litter after a carnival.

Mrs McKee beckoned her in, quickly shutting the half-glazed porch door behind them. "Oh, God! Oh, God!" she kept saying. "They were coming along, him and the son. It was rain or shine with Arthur. 'I do my job,' he'd say, 'Let others do theirs. No man can do more.'"

"Who?" Lily asked. "Who said...?"

"Arthur. Arthur the milkman. He just wanted to do his work. Protestant streets. Catholic streets. He'd say, 'A one'd give me a hard word now round here for being Protestant but I just say to them, 'Are the cows Catholic too, Mister? A wonder nobody telt me that! Ye'll be wanting Catholic milk only, will ye?' We laughed about it. And the wee lad, Malcolm. Fourteen."

Lily saw figures come up from the Catholic streets, furtively.

"Malcolm wanted a horse, God help him, and him living in a house with a tiny wee garden but Arthur just said, 'He can have a horse when he's earnt it.'"

Two young teenage boys were walking around the float, scrutinising it.

"They were waiting," Mrs McKee went on. "They must have been. They stoned the float. And they stoned the firemen who tried to get through when it crashed. The firemen were begging them to stop but...." She suddenly stumbled towards the back room.

Lily watched one boy peer in at the driver's side of the cab. He exclaimed in awe. The second boy hurried to him and together they gawped into the cab. They went still. Whatever was in there was too much for them. At last, one stretched over to the passenger seat and lifted up something dark and floppy, with even darker blotches on it.

"His jacket! The wee fella's jacket!" he gasped. "It's all blood!"

As he held it up, they both gazed at it, stricken. But the jacket did not hold its power long. Their eyes glittered. Their teeth drew back from their lips, avidly. The teenager dropped the jacket and straightened, manfully.

"C'mon," he ordered, and the two of them began to fill the crates with bottles. "C'mon!" he shouted across the road behind him and other youngsters − kids − emerged and swarmed around the float, efficiently looting it and sorting among the debris for useable bottles. The scene became more and more like a party. Lily saw several men monitoring the action from far back, half-hidden.

It was the bottles that mattered. Nobody cared about the milk.

A pool of white gathered near the blocked gutter. There would be plenty of petrol bombs made, ready for tonight. Swiftly the carcass of the float was stripped. Arthur and his son shouldn't have got in the way.

It was no good. Lily backed down the hallway. It was no good to be good, to assert normality, to reach out as best you could, to do your duty and deliver the milk. Inhuman, even your own. They'd strip you bare if they got you down. That pool of milk at the side of the road by the battered light standard and the sinking church – it was infinitely deep. How cold the eyes of men who set children to ambush a child. The road itself was a dark expanse. Stones smashed into it. There! There was the first circle around a stone's impact and the next and the next, each circle spreading further and further. How an evil act gathers force, spreading with callous ease. It has all the time in the world. Here was a ripple heading for her now, gleaming and implacable, mocking all puny efforts to go against the surge, just about to pull her under with its first voluptuous and brutal....

Something crashed behind her. Mrs McKee stood looking at a dropped milk bottle. A kettle in the kitchen beyond began to scream. Mrs McKee said, "Just a cup of tea. I thought... then I thought of wee Malcolm...." She held the bottle-top out. "I thought..." Lily took it from her and helped her to sit down.

Lily looked back up the hall. A dark seepage was insinuating itself under the porch door, crawling over the floor tiles.

She went into the kitchen. The kettle was spurting on the gas hob. Mrs McKee's voice reached her. "He was a good wee lad. He'd give you the shirt off his back."

Lily's hand clenched on the hot metal handle of the kettle and her heart roared. She filled her hand with the burning pain, letting its energy stoke her. She would not let go till she chose to. She swore, by that shirt, that she would never let herself be washed away, never give up. *I will cause ripples too.* It was love or hate, resist or drown.

She would begin by putting her arms around Mrs McKee.

THE SEA HOSPITAL

Until now I have only seen a blue like this in a stained-glass window. You know the trick: you're looking up at a window, so-called, though it doesn't let in much light – for a window. It's in some trendy, modern abstract mode so there's a lot of near-opaque, dark stuff and then – a punch of colour through the murk, a crimson, blood-gout red, pulsing at you out of the void. *Life!* it grins gleefully. *Coming to get you!*

And higher up, there'll be a blotch of unapologetic green: holly green, old and knowing green, swimming along about its own mulchy business and then, way, way up there, a cobalt, mineral but alive, shock-charged with utter blue; the heavens in a bleb of glass.

Here the sea has caught exactly that vivid, lucent colour. Between this shoreline and the island opposite, and around to the right – the passage out to Scotland – the sea is a thoroughfare of blue, bright as enamel, shivering like a pelt. I fill my eyes with it, against next winter's dearth.

We sit in Davy's conservatory: tea, cake, the amazing spring-time sea beyond the glass. We were boys together and I listen as Davy and his mother talk. They both have it, that gift of conjuring pictures. I see another house that Davy has his eye on, a house in a seaside town, not remote like this. I see a sketched-out, post-retirement life. I see the double-fronted desirability, the good sense. Davy at eighteen, circumspect. Davy at forty-eight, shrewd.

Let me adore all efforts of this kind: this planning to be content.

I adore as a man does who is amazed at a thing he can't really comprehend.

As I leave, Davy's mother sparks up about my uncle. He lived a few miles away. With the frankness of age, she says of him, *Odd wee man. Aye.*

His house was comfortless: a bilious green inside, with him sputtering around in it, a hampered, frightened spirit, hoping that jokes would do the trick. What trick? Learning to live? Like the failing comedian, doomed to ridicule or the forced laugh, he was an embarrassment; never learning how the others get it right; damaged from the start. To be with him was to be with death because he tried so frantically to keep death at bay that there was hardly room to think of anything else. He favoured jerky callisthentics and long walks that took him out past Davy's house. Did nobody ever give him just a hint at how to live? But it gets so that nobody knows where to start. So much to undo before you could build it up again.

It takes some nerve to take a stand, I think, to take a stand and... but the roof of a car is glimpsed, higher than the hedges, and here are the Missouri Yanks Davy has been expecting. How large they are in fawn chinos and roomy polo shirts. How thrilled and – yes – only just arrived at the place and they're enquiring if Davy's holiday let is for sale. Well. They're planning content. The woman hugs a pile of sheets that Davy's mother gives her. She beams. A rental week of bliss. They're planning content.

I think (as they mistake the Polish gardener for Davy's brother), I think: it takes some nerve to take a stand and take a risk and say: *You're wrong. Don't. Don't do it. Don't* (whatever the thing you're trying to tackle is) – *don't keep us all at bay with quips and riddles; don't jog in your track suit in the kitchen while you're talking – you're as doomed as the rest of us; don't think we can't see that you don't know how to let anyone love you* – I think that would be brave.

Other people's wounds. I used to think it went like this: wounds are displayed, pity evoked, poultice applied. But now I wonder if there should be a calling out – like Lazarus from the tomb; a summoning up of serum from within so that the wounded learn to live from deep within themselves. It's someone else's voice that calls but....

Parp! The Americans' huge car slots into place beside The Salt Bay door. Davy has made a ruin into a nest, tucked into the black, shallow steps of rock that face east. Such a view! The edge of Ireland's north, and Scotland seeming touchable, out at sea. And such a story. To this spot the Sons of Uisneach were lured by the false promise of a king from the sad safety of exile in Scotland, and Deirdre of the Sorrows stepped ashore among them, equally duped, equally hoping against hope. The Americans are practically fainting with awe; itching, I bet, to send the news back home. Davy's mother urges blankets *For the nights are cold yet.* Davy's quick to say, *Central Heating* as he leads them to the door.

Such a harsh remedy here, before. He'll be telling them the story there inside. How, two hundred years ago, that sea, that glinting, element they're gazing at, was rendered to astringency in the salt pans out of doors: natural basins formed in these shelves of rock. Fevers and madness were swathed in salty, saturated sheets and plunged in the whirlpool's maw – yes, a whirlpool, out there beyond. *Don't cross those rocks at night!* he'll joke, not joking. *Aye. They'd tie the patient to a chair then lower it, down into the rocky void.*

Gee, why?

Well, he'll say, *who knows, but would YOU be thinking about your symptoms in circumstances like those? A shock to the system.*

Frightening the patient back to life, d'ye think?

As a boy, I used to teeter on that brink, watching the churning suck-hole far below. Even to look was brave. But I'm on a lawn now. Safe. These gardens are a marvel: nooks and sunny spots and all the flowers that can live in such salty air. What an amount of work has gone into this, creating a pleasurable place.

The air is cooling in the swift spring twilight and the sea is navy. It ripples heavily like a bolt of serge unfurled across a counter for inspection.

Going to see my uncle – it was a penance. You'd see the curtains twitch in the house of death. He might or might not answer. You'd have to step over the gate because he kept it locked. The neighbours'd be looking, the kids in the street calling out, astonished, *Mammy! There's a man going in!* The door would open just a chink and there'd a chain-lock on. But once you were inside he'd be fizzing with manic energy, keen to show off his bargains – multiple tins of soup or how much money he'd made from burning all the family photos and selling the albums. If he stopped, he'd die. Did he even sleep? He'd pull you down if you didn't keep your head.

That's my father's family. Quick to laugh, if that's what they thought would get them by, but it struggled to reach the wary eyes. People who were always alert, knowing they were begrudged what good they got; ready to be snarled at and turned on, expecting the rebuff and the put-down. No repartee from them apart from the clinker of stored-up wrongs. Planning survival, not content.

There's laughter from The Salt Bay and hosts and guests emerge. The Yanks are beaming. Up they get into the vast car and away for supplies. I take my leave by the door that gives onto the beach where the whirlpool lurks.

From all around, colour has drained away. Ahead, the island, like a stencil on a wall, presents itself in blocks of black. The strand to the left is grey; the village it leads to, a dark mass on its promontory; beyond that, a silvery veil of sky with a hem of cold light touching the sea. I climb up on to the rickety wooden walkway that leads out to the whirlpool, over boulders and gaps. As a child, the thrill! It was a Walk To Doom, clinging to the one hand rail, daring to glance down between the cracks in the boards at the wavelets darting and retreating below. And then, a leap, to land on the great outcrop itself, a hardened, burnt-brown, pitted honeycomb of rock, thwarting every step. And the sound! A booming, threshing growl from somewhere underneath suddenly bursting up through the dark mass as a jet of white spray, grabbing the air and falling back, defeated – this time. There would always be a next!

But not for us. I know that now. There is a photograph of me as a toddler standing at this spot. I frown, all pudgy in my little bathing trunks. I frown. My hand is in my father's hand. That's all of him that the photo shows, his hand and arm. He's long, long dead.

That swaying sensation at the brink. You know?

Down in the chamber the sea rushes in and funnels and spins and races out and away, a chain of demons, roaring: *Face your worst fears, old friend. Face us and live. Hold back and die.* Such a seductive choir. I could just go, let go, give in and cease. My heavy head could droop, tipping the balance and I'd fall, slowly....

Throw me a rope, haul up on my chair! I must not drown. Must I?

Which do you fear more: sickness or health? the demons cackle and sneer.

I teeter on the edge. Fling me out now! Be merciless. Kindness can kill, keeping everything unchanged. Let the sea salt my wounds. Then, with clear eyes, I will plan my content. I will!

Who am I babbling to? Myself? I turn to look at the way I've come. The cliff that backs the strand is enormous, looming, and the sky above it starless and cold. The waves discuss the beach, over shingle, endlessly but they can't be seen. The hole behind me chuckles and thuds. I baulk at the journey back across those rocks. Then a sudden tiny brightness flares, low down by the shore, like a mercury-silver gash in the darkest of glass panes. *Life!* it giggles. *Coming to get yooooo!* The Yanks home for the night.

I have to laugh, stranded here, between that hole at my back and that cosiness ahead! And I have to laugh at myself, as I go, slipping and wavering, cursing and sploshed. Very heroic. I pitch forward and shells slit and skin my hand. Instinctively to the mouth it goes. A salty tang. Blood and sea.

When I make it off the rocks I sit down and I sob. It has to go. What? What has to go? The family skin. I have to zip it off, stepping out of it somehow. I must unwrap myself, calling myself out of the devil's maw. *That's no name for yer Granny!* my uncle's voice quips instantly, quick to belittle anything serious, anything real. *Cover it up, quick, quick, or we're all done for. The thing is never to look and see,* he advises, nervily.

No. I must look. I must see. I must choose Life that's coming to get me. Silly and tragic.

Waving in the darkness, Davy's daft, doomed, beautiful, pale, what-the-hell roses reach for the shore over his garden wall.

THROUGH BUSHES AND
THROUGH BRIARS

The Bryncysyllte Folk Festival loomed over Sinéad's summer. Dewi loved it. He checked with her, of course, that she wanted to go. Yes, yes, she assured him.

He did all the bookings, hooked up with friends, chatted about where they'd eat and what the weather would be like.

It was her voice he'd first fallen in love with. He liked to remind her of that – how astonishing it had been to hear her suddenly sing, unselfconsciously. Sitting with friends, she had simply offered a song, as she might have made any friendly gesture.

She could remember his expression. As people clapped, he sat with his mouth open and did not move for some moments. The longer she'd spent on this side of the Irish Sea the more familiar she had become with that reaction, especially from men. Clearly, over here in Wales, this proffering of songs wasn't part of their culture. Dewi was the kind of Welshman who could sing lustily enough in a rugby crowd or a congregation but this standing up on your own and just singing, with nothing but your voice, he seemed to regard as a kind of magic, particularly as he was no sort of a performer himself.

Sinéad knew lots of folk songs. At home many people did. It wasn't anything special. She had never been to a folk club in her life till Dewi took her to one. She hadn't enjoyed it – there seemed something earnest and manufactured about it – but he enjoyed seeing people pleased by her singing and she liked to please.

But pleasing him when they went home to her village had become a kind of torture. Dewi had never understood the dynamics of the sessions in her local pub. He couldn't read the interplay of status among the musicians nor the implicit structure of the evening whereas she knew how years of playing together had created an unspoken accommodation between this performer's egotism and that one's diffidence. There were standards to do but also those numbers that the group gave their best to; the ones that had an almost painful edge of musical loveliness. After one of those there would be a moment of exquisite silence before the applause, a moment in which the players and listeners were as one, in which the everyday seemed suspended. Such moments were what everyone came for. Novelty wasn't important.

What did count, then, Sinéad wondered. Some sort of beauty, she supposed. And part of that beauty was the unremarked demonstration of togetherness, for what's the song without someone to hear it? And being allowed to enter the charmed circle and contribute was a privilege. It was earned not because you were brilliant (for some of the regular contributions weren't 'good') but because you'd shown a willingness to know your place, even if that place was a lowly one; and your place was in among songs and tunes that belonged to everyone. Not 'my' song. 'Our' song. If someone, passing through, came up with an exceptional performance, they'd be acclaimed, justly, but not allowed to dominate.

Not grasping how things worked and meaning only well by pushing for her to be allowed to sing, Dewi created resentment, so when she did sing, it was often not her best and Dewi was a little disappointed. She knew you had to read the mood and there was no point in doing a sensitive lament if what the crowd wanted was a rollicker but she also knew that he wanted them to hear her voice as he liked it best, rising in a plaintive wave to break in trickling grace-notes, falling to rest before swooping up again into a new phrase. She tried to please him. She knew he didn't realise how hard it is to sing against the crowd nor what tension she felt in going against her instincts. It seemed so trivial a thing to undertake. Just a song or two.

To make things worse, there had been a general change. The crowd in the pub used to be mostly locals whose attitude set the tone for venturesome foreigners but, with the Troubles easing, tourists arrived on a truly commercial scale and Sinéad saw how the musicians chafed, year by year, as the pub morphed into an entertainment venue. Where once people had quietened to listen to them play, applauded the extra nuance, the extra spark, and offered their own contributions, this crowd now yabbered on, regardless. Piling out of Paddy wagons, they were greedy for the Irishness they thought they knew. They drowned out the subtlety this one small Ulster townland could have offered them.

The musicians were obliged to get amplification and, year on year, the repertoire stultified. The singing was no longer a pooling of experience out of common stock, filtered through an individual's voice. It became a commodity, to be consumed. Eventually even quality had no hold, for it didn't matter whether you played well or badly for this crowd as long as you played loudly enough. Dewi didn't understand what that felt like. Sinéad's difficulty with singing in the local grew till by now she was having to screw herself up to the prospect of singing there at all.

This Welsh Folk Festival wasn't quite so bad but still a struggle. The musicians circled their wagons around the pub tables and marshalled their groupies who, in turn, policed the pecking-order She didn't know why Dewi was blind to this competitiveness. She suspected an obscure but fierce egotism in herself, otherwise why would all this matter?

The previous summer, for the first time, she had consciously prepared some songs in advance instead of simply choosing something to suit the moment. She'd hoped it would ease the tension in her if she knew that she could just bring something out, sing it, have done with it and ignore the mood of the moment. For the Bryncysyllte this year she thought she'd go for *Through Bushes And Through Briars*. An English song.

She'd always intended to learn it since hearing it in a film she'd seen on tv as a child: *Far From The Madding Crowd*. "Through bushes and through briars…" She loved that opening phrase: a path beaten through obstacles. None of your casual, "As I roved out one morning fair…."

The film clip was easily found on YouTube. A Victorian country idyll. A perfect summer evening outside an English farmhouse. Luminous Julie Christie sits at the head of a long table, set for an unpretentious meal. She plays that marvel of the times, a woman boss. Seated ahead of her are a dozen men, a collection of rustic types. It's a moment of contentment among all. She is asked for a song. She complies, with simplicity. The melody is sad, with a peculiar haltingness to the tune that demands attention, perhaps because it doesn't follow the expected path.

I overheard a female
Her voice it rang so clear:
Long time have I been waiting for
The coming of my dear.

She sings with no artifice. She is a channel for the music and the sentiments it carries. They flow into the air. The poor man who loves her accompanies her on a flute. The rich man who loves her looks up to her from the foot of the table. The camera tracks down the line of faces. Each man is drawn into the song, enraptured, open-mouthed, as though he believes her to be singing only for him: the shepherd, the bailiff, the vicar, the fool. The camera gives us the rich man, alone in the frame, as he listens to the others instinctively join her in the reprise of the very last lines which are full of a bleak realism. They blend their voices with hers in an act of involuntary, voluntary, humble accession but the rich man remains un-singing, detached, as though he's thinking, *She is mine. These others merely borrow her.*

And yet, Sinéad saw, he has himself been captured somehow. She has reached in and taken him by the heart with her voice; and all, Sinéad realised now, without her meaning to. She has woken desire, without – herself – desiring.

Sinéad tried a verse. Yes, a song of unease.

Sometimes I am uneasy
And troubled in my mind
Sometimes I think I'll go to him
And tell to him my mind.

She started as she felt a hand on her shoulder. "I love your voice," Dewi said. "Carry on." She didn't want to. Yet she did what he wanted.

But if I should go to my love
My love he would say nay
If I showed to him my boldness
He'd ne'er love me again.

Even as he opened his mouth to praise her, she spoke. "I don't want to sing at the Folk Festival." Her daring startled her. What would he do now? His grip on her shoulder tightened.

"You don't mean that," he said. "Go on. How does it end?"

"That's it. That's all the singer could remember when a collector overheard him in a pub."

"Add a few words yourself," he laughed. He shook her slightly. "Go on."

Yes. Her back stiffened.

"Dewi," she whispered. "I didn't mean it to be like this."

COWARD

"Brother."

"Wife," Maggie said.

The nurse told them that she would take them to a waiting room and that a doctor would come and explain Aidan's condition fully. As soon as she left them Maggie went off to the toilet and did not reappear for a long time. They had arrived at the Intensive Care Unit at almost the same moment: he from Belfast, and she from somewhere in the Midlands — Birmingham, he thought.

She hadn't been tidying her hair, Niall noted with disapproval when she came back, for it was still half caught up at the back of her head and hung round her pale face in long black strands. Her stone-coloured raincoat, which she still wore, her large black bag — she was the colour of newsprint.

When they were given a briefing (for that's how she seemed to treat the doctor's account of what had happened to Aidan — the pub encounter, an attack, a single blow, felling Aidan to the tiled floor) she had asked terse questions and listened so intently that Niall could almost see the words forming up in her mind. Sentences. Paragraphs. "Inoperable acute subdural haemorrhage complicated by extensive intra-cerebral bleeding secondary to alcoholic cirrhosis." He watched her note this down meticulously. They both understood that Aidan was going to die. The doctor left them, saying that they would be brought to Aidan's bedside shortly.

"Are you staying?" Niall asked her abruptly, irritated by that coat.

She was still wearing it when they were left alone with Aidan in a curtained cubicle. Niall had seen this set-up before, on tv. It looked exactly as it ought to and he had a role to play: the sombre, steady eldest brother. He even knew he wasn't supposed to obsess over the monitors or fret about procedure. The dedicated staff were sure to be doing everything they could, while keeping their complex personal lives on hold. He expected to be overwhelmed by information. That's what everyone said about these situations. The unpredictable element was Maggie but even in respect to her he felt fore-armed. He watched her take her coat off, look around briefly for somewhere to put it, then drape it over the end of the bed. At once he snatched it up, saying pointedly, "I'll get another chair." He disappeared to find one and returned, placing the chair ostentatiously away from the bed and putting the coat over its back. She sorted through the contents of her bag, as though catching up on a small routine task. Clearly, she was not going to make this easy.

Niall was uncomfortable. They ought to talk but he had seen how she stiffened at his shocked remarks to the doctor about the attack on Aidan. Yes, he had said conventional things: *When? How? What next?* Was there anything new to say when a brother had been assaulted in a pub? And, of course, he wanted to know who'd done it? Had Aidan brought it on himself? That was a possibility.

Maggie had found him wanting in the conversation with the doctor. But she always had. Well, she wasn't going to get away with sitting there being superior. What could he begin with? Something insultingly mundane? *How are you? How's the job?* He wasn't sure which paper she worked for. One he didn't read.

"I thought you'd be full of questions," he found himself saying.

She raised an eyebrow. "You haven't seen Aidan for a long time."

"And you have?"

"We keep in touch! The odd phone call."

"When? When was the last one?"

"Last week," he bridled.

"Oh?"

"Aidan phoned to say he was coming over to Belfast. 'Get the weekend over,' he said, 'and I'll be home.' He should have been with us today. Ma...." In front of this Englishwoman he checked himself from saying 'Mammy'. "My mother's very ill. Very ill," he stressed, pointedly. "She wanted to see him."

"Never waste a good deathbed."

As he gasped, she stood, snatched up her coat, said, "I'll be back." and was already reaching into her handbag. Still a smoker, Niall thought. The curtain billowed in her wake.

Had Aidan heard that bitchery? But Aidan was motionless.

Maggie returned. Niall went to the toilet. She left when he came back. She returned. They sat in silence together.

A medic came in from time to time, did this or that procedure, and each time Niall forgot to breathe. Was this going to be the action that saved Aidan, the crucial intervention in his life? There had been so many efforts over the years of boozing. The hope and promises. The return to zero. Maggie. Aidan had wasted years of her life. Aidan told him she said that the night she left for good.

But her column! *Living with an Alcoholic.* That she could sit down and methodically craft something out of their misery! 'Tellin' our business about the streets,' Mammy called it. Plenty of meat there! The troubled Belfast childhood; the Irish Catholic family numerous enough to disgust English tastes. Maggie had pinned Aidan down on page after page for the entertainment of strangers: the decline, by fits and starts, of a brilliant, fearless jour-

nalist; her keeping the show on the road, sobering him up and filling in for him; his tearful promises; his sudden, ruinous
extravagances; his self-deception. There was a story there, all
right, and she hadn't missed the chance to tell it. Self-righteous
cow!

From the other side of the bed, she returned Niall's gaze and held
it, before coolly looking away, at the monitor, the ceiling, her nails.

"Why did you come?" he demanded.

She shut her eyes. "Because...." She opened them and looked
at him unflinchingly. "I loved him. I don't *now*, of course but it's
tidier if someone's here with him, isn't it?"

"You made enough out of him anyway!"

"Fuck off," she said calmly. "I didn't think any of you would
be here. But you overcame your scruples, did you? Turned up for
talks?"

"God forgive you!"

"Oh! Please!"

A nurse pulled the curtain aside, frowning. "OK?"

"Yes, yes." Niall reddened. Maggie smirked at this. The nurse
vanished. "You never gave him a chance!" he hissed.

She snorted. "If he'd sobered up life would have been boring.
That's what he couldn't face. Your brother couldn't handle an ordi-
nary, daily slog. He had to have more and more... *something*.
Something had to always be happening! Yeah. You know that."

He turned away from her. She stood. "Do you want a coffee?"
He shook his head, incredulous that she could ask. She shrugged
and left.

Niall looked at Aidan's thin fingers. Skin and bone. Stubble on
his poor, battered face. His mouth all wounded. Oh, Jesus!

"Stubborn bastard!" Niall said aloud. Aidan could always hold
out against anyone.

When they were teenagers, Aidan's laughter would be heard from behind a bedroom door, impervious to teasing and attempted interruptions; the radio on; people with English voices making Aidan laugh. Later he'd do the sketches for them, announcing, "Wait'll ye hear this!" and he'd deliver the lines, perfect accent and all. The skits didn't always seem funny to Niall but Aidan soaked them all up. Words. Words. He'd get hot and bothered about reports in the local papers. Who cares, Niall would demand, about what gets said *after* the event? It was the thing itself that mattered, and didn't Aidan think they had enough to cope with, living on the front line, every other night a running riot, sirens, bullets? "Nobody cares!" Niall had said, time and again.

"I'll make them care. I'll tell it like it is!" Aidan had finally declared.

"You?" and as soon as the contemptuous word was uttered Niall had seen the hurt flood Aidan's eyes and his eyelids drop in a peculiar, slow, shuttering blink, long enough for them both to know they were seeing the same thing, the one particular night.

There it was, the bed they shared in the smaller front bedroom. Two younger brothers were stacked in a bunk bed. Other brothers and sisters were in the bigger front room. When there was shooting, Niall would hustle the two wee ones into the back bedroom with Mammy and Daddy and return to bed to wait it out. Aidan would lie still, apparently asleep.

Night after night in that bedroom, Aidan would pretend to be unconscious but Niall felt constantly stretched, sending his attention out into the urban un-darkness to sift information from its sounds. He had learned how to tell when an army patrol was approaching. All casual noise – a walker's cough, the clink of milk bottles being put out – would drain away into a tense absence and resume once the soldiers had passed. He could judge when a night's climax had been reached from how the soldiers sounded: while things were still on the climb he could hear their things rather than them – the scrape of a boot as someone eased his position; the incidental *tink* of metal on metal; a radio squawk. Later it would be a sigh, a laugh, a belligerent, ostentatious fart.

He hated being in this corner bedroom on the end of a terrace, exposed on two sides, for there was a small window in the gable-end. It was like being on the prow of a ship forever facing into danger. He braced himself through every night, holding himself ready for the moment when he would have to do something. He was sure he would. Something would happen and he would have to act, to save the family. Why it wasn't his father's job to do that he never considered. He was certain it was his. And there lay Aidan, oblivious. Wilfully.

On that night, a very hot night in August, Aidan slept as usual against the back wall opposite the front window and Niall lay on the outside of the bed. He watched the lights of an armoured car swing across the curtains. There were still hours to go before daylight. The room was chokingly warm. Niall went to the window and eased the curtains aside a little. Across the road, heavy trees pressed against the far side of the long, high wall of the city park, their black masses paralysed by the heat; so stiff they looked like cut-outs.

There were occasional shots. Niall listened to feet thudding past only yards away on the pavement. Shouts and curses came through the walls as an army patrol hugged the gable-end down the side street that ran off the main road. Niall sweated from more than the heat. He shepherded the wee ones out of their bunks and into the back bedroom, carrying one and trailed by the stumbling, sleepy other.

He got back into bed beside Aidan. As long as Niall could interpret the sounds outside he felt he was somehow in control. He could tell himself that he knew what was happening. But on this night, he could read no meaning into what he was hearing. There was a distant chaos outside. A riot gathering in the offing? Niall felt something slipping inside him. He grabbed Aidan's arm in the bed. "Listen!" he urged. But Aidan resolutely absented himself, eyes shut.

A bullet pinged off the edge of the front window frame and Niall cried out, instinctively ducking away. When he opened his eyes his face was almost touching Aidan's and he could see the frissons of tension in his brother's forehead, the effort he was making to not see, not hear.

It wasn't fair. Aidan shouldn't escape like this, leaving Niall alone. "Wake up!" Niall yelled. "Wake up!" but Aidan didn't move. "I know you're awake. I know you are!" Niall insisted. Nothing. But then Niall felt something on his leg, something warm, and a smell, unmistakeable.

Niall leapt out of the bed, furious. "Loser!" he shouted. "Coward!" No reaction. Wild with frustration, he ran downstairs and out into the back yard. He was shocked to find himself crying. Aidan was getting away with something – something – while he was having to take all the burden. It wasn't fair. Why was it he who had to be brave while Aidan 'slept'? Why should he be the only one who had to see what was going on?

Niall's contemptuous 'you' had echoed between them as they had both emerged from the intimate, night-time life that Niall had dragged into the light. Aidan had said, "Aye, well." He had looked Niall full in the face. "Aye, well. We'll see."

And now Aidan lay so still that Niall urged, "You're not asleep.

You can hear me, can't you?" No answer.

"You're hurting him, I should think." Maggie's voice broke on Niall and he realised he was squeezing Aidan's hand white. He let go. She was looking curiously at him, sipping from a plastic cup. "I thought you didn't like him. That's what he always told me. Though, oddly enough, he said it's because of you he stuck with journalism. I never got that, really."

"Could you *please*..." Niall burst out. "This isn't the place, or the time. This should be..." but he couldn't go on. He couldn't say 'holy' to this woman, though it should be a holy time. She couldn't know how often they had prayed about this moment, as a family. The Rosary every day. 'Pray for us now and at the hour of our death'. If this was Aidan's hour, then it ought to be holy. "We should get a priest," he said.

"No. Aidan wouldn't have wanted that."

"Yes, he would!"

"No. And before you rant on, I'm his wife."

The trump card.

"God, it was a hard day he met you!" he snarled.

"You *think*? What do you know? You self-righteous, uptight ... *teacher!* You never encouraged him. Never gave him a word of praise."

"That's not...."

"Sanctimonious, patronising. You made him feel small, no matter what he did. I hated your visits because he'd always drink more after you left – to get rid of the taste!" she hissed.

"He'd never have said...."

"He thought it. We're married, remember?"

Yes. Maggie as a bride, almost smothered in the wedding photos among the tribe of Donnellys; her own thin parents insignificant and strained-looking. Aidan's wife. Aidan, he thought, with a sudden sense of wonder, has been inside this woman.

"You didn't know him like I did," she insisted.

"I did!" But, of course, she was right. He couldn't know the intimacy of their marriage and she couldn't know the life they'd led as kids, packed close like cubs in a den – a world away from her tidy upbringing by a mother always in pastels and a dad who played golf.

"And you Donnellys," she went on. 'Oh, you can't say this. You can't say that.' I'll say what I like, write what I like, about my life – our lives."

"There are things that shouldn't be said outside the home – things it's not decent to tell other people."

"Because we have to keep up a front? Aidan wasn't like that. You don't get that, do you? He wanted to get behind things. He wanted to turn the spotlight on...."

"Not on himself!"

A nurse swept into the cubicle, remonstrating. Maggie pushed past her and disappeared. Niall would have followed Maggie but the nurse stopped him, saying, emphatically, "You only have so much time."

There'd be no priest, then. No deathbed blessing. No forgiveness of sins. No readying for the journey. Aidan shouldn't die like this. Even that time on the doorstep there had been... words, at least. Niall subsided into his chair.

He and Aidan had had a row. In the kitchen. Niall had three empty milk bottles in his right hand, his fingers stuffed into their necks. Aidan was persisting with a mad plan to interview a paramilitary. "Who do you think you are?" Niall demanded. "You're seventeen!" But Aidan was adamant and suddenly Niall's envy had overwhelmed him – that Aidan, who pissed himself in the night, could want something so much and believe that he could get it! Didn't he know life was about cutting your dreams down to size?

Niall, fuming, strode up the hallway to put the milk bottles out, wrenched open the front door – and all but fell over a soldier crouched on the doorstep. The milk bottles crashed to the ground. The soldier swore, shouldered Niall off – a bullet! Smashing off the bricks by their heads! From the trees opposite. The soldier made to drop into position on the front path but a shot caught him, flinging him back against the door as Niall slammed it forward. Niall fought the soldier's weight. A wordless, total struggle. The soldier's gasp. Time only to act, not think. Pure will: to shut out. To shut out. Out.

Niall felt himself pulled sharply backwards. Aidan tugged the door open. The soldier toppled across the threshold, blood pumping from his throat.

Aidan dropped to his knees, pressing his hands over the welling blood. Their mother ran up the hallway. She stepped unhesitatingly over the body so she could look the young man in the face. "Oh, Jesus," she said. "Oh, Sweet Jesus." She smiled at him, holding his startled eyes. "Oh, son. I'm here. I'm here now. It'll be all right." He died.

"You fuckers!" Aidan yelled towards the unmoving trees, "I'll get you!"

Niall clutched at Aidan who, checked, looked down at Niall's hands, astounded. They tussled for a moment till Aidan, with an angry cry of disgust, broke free and ran into the house. The hallway phone was bloodied in his grip and his gaze fixed burningly on Niall as, in a cold, urgent voice, he demanded an ambulance.

Niall groaned. He had held Aidan back. Even then. He put his face in his hands. His skin had already picked up a faint hospital taint.

He – his body – would never forget the wrenching, backward momentum as Aidan pulled him away from the door. He could feel Aidan's bulk pushing in between him and what must not be let in.

But Aidan had opened that door. Fearlessly. No – despite fear.

And Aidan alone had seen what Niall's choice had been.

Niall looked at Aidan's ashen face. In that battered head, in that memory, was a record of Niall's shame.

"Oh, Jesus!" Niall laid his forehead against Aidan's arm. *You never once said it. You never confronted me with it, but I hated you more because you were afraid, but you did things anyway. On the telly. In the desert. In the back streets. You went for them, whoever they were. And I was glad every time you failed at home, behind the scenes. Every time you let yourself down. And there was Maggie's catalogue of your petty little failures and I was glad.* "I was glad," he said aloud. "Sweet Jesus!"

Maggie's voice rang out. "I said no prayers."

"But I wasn't...!"

"You can stop that cant. He told me, you bastard. He told me how he wanted it to be at the end, what he wanted me to say. Do you think he didn't know things might end like this?"

"Maggie, I wasn't praying. I swear. I was thinking how much courage he has. I was...."

"No!" She was anguished now. The nurse returned. "Get him out of here!"

"Both of you," the nurse urged, "security will have to intervene if you...."

Barely aware the nurse had spoken, Niall insisted, "But, Maggie, you don't know. You don't know how it was – how brave he was."

Maggie recoiled. "Brave?" She stepped close to Aidan and bent towards him. She said in a clear, hard voice, "You are such a coward. Aidan, do you hear that? You're a coward."

"Maggie!" Niall cried.

She held up a hand to fend Niall off. "Aidan, you wouldn't save yourself. Coward!"

The nurse exclaimed and reached towards Maggie, her other arm gesturing in Niall's direction to two male staff who arrived ready for confrontation. They eyed Niall and moved towards him. He ducked his head and held up his hands in a placating gesture – anything rather than be taken away. He had to stop Maggie.

But she carried on. "Aidan, you've been the worst sort of coward. Anything outside yourself, you could face but you wouldn't look yourself in the eye. *No, blot that out. Quick!* And you made me watch you slip deeper and deeper and you wouldn't stretch out your hand. You coward."

"No!" Niall cried, lunging towards her. He was grabbed on both sides. He resisted with all his strength till Maggie looked at him and said, "It's the truth." Niall suddenly gave way, collapsing backwards in the men's grip.

Through the tangle of limbs and protesting voices he heard her say, "I promised, I'd tell him the truth." As Niall was hoisted to his feet she insisted, "That's what he cared about. He couldn't live up to it but he wanted to hear it – at the end. 'Tell me then,'" he said.

"Stop now," said one of the men to Niall. "It doesn't help. If you want to stay, calm down."

"Maggie," he pleaded, "let me tell him…. I want him to know that…."

But she was weeping. "You thought you were shit, Aidan."

"No, Aidan! Not you!" Niall cried.

"OK, mate. Better off out of here just now." Niall was pulled through a set of doors, hearing Maggie say, "… that you didn't deserve..." as they shut behind him.

"It was me!" Niall shouted.

"Course it was," said one of the men.

"Time and place," said the other.

Niall was taken into a room and spoken at. He said nothing, for nothing that was said got through to him.

SAFETY FIRST

Juliet, sitting on the beach in her swimsuit, kept her eyes closed, the better to enjoy the wonderful, precious heat, the amazingly present heat, of a summer day − a summer day with no spiteful breeze, no capricious clouding-over but a steady, powerful, sunny beneficence so rare as to be miraculous. On this northern coast the sea was usually grey-blue cold and the air damp throughout July and August. "I could be a different person," she thought, "if it was always like this."

She felt warm grains of sand between her toes. She wiggled them and pressed her feet down hard. There would be dark beige mounds there if she were to inspect the effect but she knew how they would look, like miniature Saharas.

How often did she think about the undersides of her feet, those shy, strong, tensile bridges on which her whole body weighed? They were beautifully engineered. She had seen once, years ago, on television, how a whole great office block was kept in place by the precise tension between the concrete structure's immense weight and the upward thrust of a steel bow held at a calculated arc deep inside it. The challenge involved in demolishing the building, after damage in some conflict, was how to take it down without the bow springing out of place as its load was lightened. She had imagined a thrilling, though deadly, fountain of blocks and girders and struts and bolts if the job were botched but she never got to see how it turned out. Her Dad had thought it boring and switched channels.

She retained the image of the smart, modern building, so solid-seeming, so suddenly redundant and vulnerable, both a victim and a threat to those who intended to sweep it away. They hadn't expected to be wanting rid of it so soon and it hadn't wanted to go. She could see – as though she had really seen it – that steel arch hidden beneath the functional exterior and she imagined it as having a giant wing-nut at each end which someone would have to slacken off bit by bit so as to remove, floor by floor, the weight that would otherwise have burst everything apart. Safety first.

But today, she was stocking up on sun, lifting her unseeing face, willing the hot light in at every pore. Being here was so effortless. In weather like this there was no resigned making the best of weak spurts of sunshine between clouds that unfurled and furled themselves like sodden awnings; no stoical layering of summer clothes, their jolly colours and flimsy fabrics ridiculous in the challenging reality of a British summer. This – this heat – was how it was meant to be.

Matthew was close by her, sitting, with knees drawn up, on a beach towel. She considered how he looked – she didn't need to see. She could feel sun lotion liquefying on her face, back and closed eyelids as her inner gaze moved from his eyes to his smile, to his shoulders and elbows and hands, his beautiful feet, whose tendons, when flexed, made delicate channels run down towards the gaps between his toes. She groaned inwardly: to think of detail like that was evidence of only one thing.

She too was sitting with knees to her chest. She rested her forehead on them. She could hear an ice cream van's metallic jangle, faintly, from beyond the dunes. The staccato of children's shouts and squeals, from the shoreline and closer by, was benignly insignificant beneath the immense dome of unblemished blue sky. "So much room!" she thought. "And we are so small."

She pressed the bridge of her nose into the cleft between her knees, contracting her world, helmeted in flesh-scented darkness, and there she projected a screening of Matthew's perfect legs: the pure escarpment from the knee down the shin; the full calf curving into the complex engineering of the ankle; the cuppable heel.

Her eyes still shut, she surveyed the beach. She saw the two of them sitting there on the towels, among a flotsam of the others' clothes and pails and sun cream and spades and the little stash of watches, jewellery, wallets and car keys. Children and adults were strewn across the sand and water as though spilled out at random. Room for everyone. A parent scooped up a straying, wailing toddler. Teenagers were strung out at intervals, splishing across the thin fans of water displaying and retracting themselves at the sand's edge. A solitary figure here and there trod with care among pebbles, head-down, self-absorbed. A few others squatted over rock pools that were slowly shrinking under the ruthless attention of the sun which had already dealt with the sea, ironing it flat.

The distribution of people seemed random. Bonds were loosened and dissolving in the heat and in the promising possibilities of the far-reaching highway of the strand. But, she thought with pain, come a cooling, come the approach of evening, and the bonds would contract back into place, the belongings be searched for and bagged up, the families re-assembled, and the ritual of leaving the beach be enacted in rinsings, re-clothings, cajolings, regrets and teasings and the trek back to the cars and the moving on to bedtime, to tomorrow.

While she stayed like this, cocooned in the heat and in her own body, she could hold on to Matthew, by doing nothing. There was nothing to be done. They could not touch and what could they speak about? They could not look at each other because that would be to speak. They must sit, veiled chaperones, the one of the other. There could be no grief, for that would reveal a loss.

A sudden shadow fell on her: her husband, asking, "You got enough cream on?" He tapped her on the shoulder with a plastic bottle which she took, squinting up at him. He brought with him a briny tang, the cold perfume of the sea, and a flitter of droplets spun off him as he slapped his limbs into warmth. She dolloped some cream carelessly into one hand and slapped it to her face unthinkingly; thinking, in fact, of darkness, of just ceasing to be, of not having to live without....

Tears poured from her eyes, blinding her, gushing like arterial blood and rightly, rightly, she thought in bewilderment. Her eyes were speaking for her! How...? She had meant to give nothing away, to leave the beach and Matthew without complaint or self-indulgence, to snap back into line and count her blessings and grieve alone but she was weeping like a Magdalen, huge teardrops hitting the sand. Her hands were hindered by their slick of sun cream. She gasped and stood. Her eyes were on fire. She rubbed her hands frantically in the towel but that merely added sand to the mix. Sightless, she ran towards the sound of the sea, towards its wetness which would wash her free.

She wrung her hands in the wavelets. She rubbed them along her sides. She scrubbed at her eyes but no good. She plunged on, head under, striking out and she opened her burning eyes to the salty, bubbling undertow. One pain drives out another! But she was shocked by the cold grip of the sea. Under the surface, it sniggered. It was the sort that would have her, if she let it, just because it could. It tumbled her with a casual cruelty so that she had to fight to come up for air, facing the beach. Her husband stood in the shallows, looking out towards her, at once anxious and exasperated. Whatever he was shouting didn't reach her. Matthew had remained far back, knowing his place. She bewailed his good sense! He was not the sort to act impulsively, dashing forward with unconcealed concern, opening her husband's eyes.

She would wade back, be admonished, brusquely comforted and corralled again. She stopped in thigh-high water, feet planted against the bullying swell. Her husband waved her in impatiently. Beyond him Matthew stood and she faced him under the sun's hot scrutiny. She recognised that he and she would hold their pain in place till it evaporated. No explosion. A dismantling by silent, invisible stages. Many, many days.

THE SCALE

Today I couldn't smile. Today she went too far − even for her. Mair. She's malice and nastiness wrapped up in a tatty cardigan. Does she sit there, all day, on her own, brewing these things up? Or do they just pop out, horrible little spurts of horrible…. Oh, God. I am going to sit with my head on the steering-wheel for two minutes. I'm already late, late, late for the next call. And I'll have to go back in to her, once I've calmed down. I stormed out. Have I got the keys? Yes.

Calmly, Lisa. Take it calmly. Perspective. Go back a few steps. Back to this morning.

I knew what Bethan wanted to hear. *It'll be fine*, I said. *Would they be sending us in if it wasn't safe?* Well, tell you what, if there was another reliable way to earn money, I wouldn't be here. But me, her, all of us got family to keep, so that's what I said and off we went on our rounds. My boys are grown. But not secure – Rhys is on furlough and Owen's job's gone. And that disgusting old bitch knew how to put her finger on just….

No. Calmly. Take it calmly.

If we didn't go to Mair, me, and Bethan and the others, who would? Her son's a dud. A district nurse called yesterday, visor and mask and all. We looked at each other stupid. Me with just a plastic apron and gloves. Neither of us said anything.

It's me who could do with looking after now, it is, sitting with my forehead on my steering-wheel. Of all my ladies and gents is Mair the worst of them? She is. Worse than Mrs Jenkins who cries all the time. Worse than Benjy Thomas who's angry at everyone and everything. They're just difficult. But Mair... she's... poisonous. You always know which of the girls have been with her because they're fit to burst, to lash out. For God's sake, look at the state she's landed *me* in!

Thursday, she wet the bed, deliberately. Friday, she let on to have dementia. "Whah?" she kept saying to everything, and then, suddenly, posh-like, "Did ewe speak?" She knows this sort of stuff delays me. I'll pay for it. Delighted, she was. Her little victory. Talk about *her* blood-pressure.

But today, oh, today.... she says, "I'm on strike!" I ignore that. "Like the miners!" she yells. "I got my rights, I have."

"You striking for better pay, Mair?" I say, as I lift the container out of her commode.

"Better conditions," she shouts after me as I head for the toilet. "Better service, like, innit." Oh, right. "A dog's life, I lead. I deserve better at my age. I'm *pre*-NHS, I am." I come back in. "You lot don't know you're born. Everything on a plate. I deserve better. I was there, I was! Nineteen-eighty-four. Miners' Strike." Really? I don't remember her. "You wouldn't remember," she snorts.

"Mair, I'm sixty. Of course I remember!"

A strike pits your power against somebody else's, so Mair won't lift an arm to be dressed, won't open her mouth for me to do the few teeth she's got left. I go off to the kitchen and when I come back, there she is, eyeing me from between her fingers. Moaning. A strike only works if there's somebody to notice it but who's to see Mair's great stand? Me and the other carers, in twenty-minute slots. "Still on strike, then, Mair?" I say, trying to turn it towards a joke. "Going on the picket line, you'll be, next." Her breakfast untouched. "Hunger-strike, is it?" I say, though I've spotted a packet of digestives peeping out from under her cushion.

"Aye." She's laughing now. "Hunger strike. That's right."

"What's so funny, Mair?".

"Oh, that's a good one, that is."

"You trying to slim down, is that it?"

Giggling, "Like your Owen. Your boy." Sniggering, "He could lose a bit. Your mongol."

She squinted up at me, grinning, knowing she'd hurt me, wanting to see how much damage she'd done. I had to get out of there or I'd have hit her, strangled her.

Owen! Always my soft spot, my weakness. Owen. As different to Mair as it's possible to be.

Well, it's me who's on strike, then! Let's hear it for me, the old song: *Union miners, stand together. Do not heed the bosses' tale. Keep your hands upon your wages, and your eyes upon the scale.*

Dad. I'm glad you're dead. All the way through the strike, and after, my God, you fought. And lost. But you could look back and know you'd done what you could. Never shirked. Held the line. Proud. And a lot came from those times. Women organising and speaking up. I was twenty-three, twenty-four. Already had Rhys. 'Do you see, Lisa, what WE can do?' What people can do together. But, Dad, things are different now.

Just another minute. I'll stay just another minute. What's the sun doing over there? Chasing something across the mountain. Like Penrhys mountain. I was eleven. The Isolation Hospital in flames. The firemen setting it alight. You took me to see it happening, Dad. Exciting. Scary. They burnt the pox out of it, out of the very earth. The flames, devouring the bad stuff.

Smallpox in the Rhondda. The carrier had come over from Pakistan. They took him to Penrhys. It's so high above the Valley, up in the pure air. You knew the family in Ferndale where that poor young mother lay in an open coffin for days so people could pay their respects – nobody knew it was smallpox had killed her. Then her sister died of it. I was a toddler then. You told me how frightened people were. How had it reached Ferndale? Was it blown down from Penrhys on the wind? And what if it got into the mine? Would people drop dead in the dark?

You said they called for the Valleys to be sealed off, isolated from the rest of the world. And the infection seemed to die down, then come back, and nurses and doctors risking their lives to look after the patients. Health Inspectors chasing down contacts. Vaccinations. Nearly a million in south Wales.

A man flies from Pakistan. Catches a train to Cardiff in nineteen-sixty-two. A man flies from China to Italy…. Patient Zero, they call him now.

We have no vaccine. And no PPE, or not enough to spare for the likes of me. I go from house to house, like a carrier. And no testing. How do I know I haven't already got it? But, surely, if it was all that risky, something would have been done by now? 'Oh, come on, Lisa, *fach!*' I hear you, Dad. 'Never assume. Ask Who gains? Who loses?' But ask who? I used to be a fighter. And then Owen came along and you can't have a child like him and not know what it's like to be at the back of the back of the queue. All my fight went into him, inching him forward towards what he deserved. Gareth buggered off.

And besides, I had hope back then. Now everything's gone global. You can't get at the people who count. And here I am in a little country, with little money and Owen to think of, and Rhys and his kids, and all day I lift people up and soothe them down and try not to worry about losing a shift, propping up one shaky old life after another as best I can.

I have to go back in to Mair. It'll be in and out. Quick as I can make it.

Key in the door.

She's on the floor. She's not shamming. She's terrified. She can't speak. I whip out my phone, do everything I'm supposed to and keep the line open. I'm kneeling beside her. How long will they be? What do I do now? Her eyes are fixed on me. Yes, you need me now, don't you? You'd do anything for me, now that I'm all you have. Just you and me now, Mair. You understand me. You're petrified. Good. You don't deserve pity. You had none for Owen. I could just let you lie there. You don't want me to, though, do you? No. You want me to have a heart. You want me to care. You stuck the knife in my son but you want me to save you. That's the bargain, the unfair bargain, isn't it? Just like we get the crappy wages because what we do isn't important – taking care of you isn't important. You're not important, Mair. You're just a number. The only little bit of power you've got is bossing me around and shitting on Owen because you think you're better than him. You see what they've done? The weak against the weak keeps the strong strong.

Christ! I take her hand before I'm swept away. There was a banner: *Your Fight Is Our Fight.* I start to sing, *A miner's life is like a sailor's 'board a ship to cross the wave. Every day his life's in danger yet he ventures, being brave.*

And she's with me, somehow, so I carry on. All the verses. And back to the beginning. And again. I am keeping her going. I am fighting off despair and bitterness. I am standing in line. Arm in arm. *Keep your hand upon the banner and your eyes upon the scale.* The team comes in through the open door, uniformed, PPE'd, efficient. I stand up. Though now nobody can stand arm in arm. And there's things you never had to fight, Dad. Trump. Climate change. The worst recession in history.

I am so tired. But it's Mrs Jenkins next. And all her tears. Let's put my heart on the scale. Let's see what it's worth.

PATTERN

She has been buried in a corner of an ordinary field newly annexed to the churchyard. I'm glad. The plot nestles in a crook of hedge. Cows graze beyond it and there's a farmyard tang on the breeze. Good. She was herself natural, you'd say. Wholesome.

I'm glad she's not in the main cemetery. Its layout has gone wrong. Blatant white concrete paths have been imposed in a grid and the hillocky green graves bullied into this rigid pattern of rectangles and sharp edges.

Maybe under a powerful sun, in Greece or Puglia, such paths would bleach into a radiance, a shimmering ground-haze blending marble and stone – all matter – into a white heat of grassless, mudless purity but here, where grass-blades stoop under the weight of showers, greenness wants to sway in ripples of shadow and brief, bright warmth.

The paths direct visitors towards the dead with the colourless efficiency of airport walkways: *This Way To Departures*. It's unkind to counter the prodigality you can smell around you and will have seen in the church whose sanctuary is lined in golden tendrils and sky-blue vistas – stone as foliage and air. Italians did that, a hundred years ago, lavishing imagination on plain walls in Antrim, piece by glittering piece.

She is like that now, carefully placed. I think she is an emerald, of the darkest green. She will never be un-beautiful.

She, our young doctor, studied Death on our behalf, shielding us, or easing us – those for whom the balance tipped too far – into the greater life she assured us of. Death ran towards her, opening all his secrets.

We flock slowly around the grave, figures detaching and uncoupling, re-joining, leaving, returning for the last look: a patterning of people whose design disperses in a slow drift – to food, homes, sleep, tomorrow.

It's only the focus widening, though. A twist to the lens and the pieces will leap to their place. Our pattern holds.

She will never be alone.

SUGARED ALMONDS

Mary sat down suddenly among the sugared almonds. They stretched away to either side of her on this part of the beach: pale lavender, a dusty pistachio green, faint pink, blue-grey. Among them, here and there, lay large, white, oval stones, the size of her hand, their surface glistening a little, as though they were made of sugar. Her daily walk had been pleasant recently in the summery weather but today on the radio Alan Titchmarsh had warned of frost in May, advising fleece cover for bedding plants. She would have to start taking an interest in the garden. Apparently, with gardening centres opening it was time to…. whatever. Everything seemed a burden even though there was plenty of time to do it in. And she had a great Deputy Head. Marvellous, how Alison had stepped up. Basics in place, of course, Mary thought with satisfaction. A well-run school was a well-run school whatever happened. A sound foundation to meet the crisis. She had even relished some aspects of it – the thinking on your feet, the pushing back against Department bullies. Had she enjoyed it too much? Had she been distracted? Andy too had gone on working. The job he loved.

She tugged her coat around her. She used to like catching the six o'clock evening news. Now she escaped it. Monday's headline had been so…. No, she wouldn't think about it.

The beach was empty. A keen breeze. Sugared almonds. Andy had exclaimed over them the first time she had brought him here. He had picked up one of the smooth little pebbles and put it to his tongue. "Salty."

"Well," she'd said, tartly, "what did you expect? A mouthful of sugar?" But her blush had betrayed her apparent brusqueness. She'd been on edge that afternoon.

She picked up and weighed a handful of the pebbles: mauve, flour-white, even pale gold. Yes, that afternoon, he wouldn't have known that inviting him to walk on the beach was, for her, the equivalent of tearing her clothes off and belly-dancing across the sand. She had hardly ever had a boyfriend. She noticed that qualification. She was given to aiming for exactness of expression – years of encouraging it in pupils. A few awkward near-misses with boys. So shamingly… inefficient… yes, that was it. Efficient generally, she hadn't had the happy knack with men. And they were very young men, she acknowledged, looking back from her fifty-four years. But at the time! At the time, of course, it was all so disappointing, or so she had tried to console herself, though, in her heart, it had been herself she'd found wanting. The qualities of discipline that made her successful as a student, the ambition that, later, would serve her well in her career, seemed to work against her with men. She had had no idea how to get what she wanted; had even found it hard to accept that she did want… it, whatever that was. Marriage. Sex. Men found her overly serious. But it *was* serious. It was your whole life, wasn't it?

Your whole life. Such dreadful angst the young go through, made worse by that end-of-the-world feel a beach can acquire on a cold evening, when the future stretches ahead as empty as the shore – as a girl, she had walked along here, unhappily trying to come to terms with her conviction that no one would ever want her.

She ran her thumb over a pale little nugget, as dingy as a rubber a child has treasured in a pencil case. Andy's first visit to this beach had been Andy allowed into her territory. She remembered wondering, *how has it got to this?* But she had known exactly.

Her first, temporary, teaching job had been in the city and that meant catching a bus from the village to the depot where she changed for the main service. He had often been driving that city-bound bus and she had paid him no more attention than she ever gave to a bus driver. Somehow, he had impressed himself on her without appearing to do anything. He hadn't even spoken to her. It had been his smile, ticket by ticket, journey after journey. There had been no pressure in that smile, nothing 'forward', as her mother would have put it, but Andy could make a smile go a long way. When she'd been sickening for the flu his smile had been full of concern and when, one day, in the summer term, she had got on the homebound bus with her arms full of flowers from the children, his smile had shared her pleasure. She had begun to fear that this level of exchange might go on forever and that fear had shown her that she was hoping for something more. She was hooked. That smile going on forever − smiled for her − was exactly, and almost all, that she wanted. So it had been she who had begun their conversations: *the traffic; thank you; see you again; lovely weather; yes, sun burnt.*

She passed the nondescript pebble from one hand to the other. Her hands were cold. She looked at the sea, a longish stone-throw away. It was in neutral, idling under a steely sky. On the last day of that term, she had lingered when they reached the depot so as to be the last passenger off the bus. She couldn't leave it till the homeward journey because that was no more than a descent of the steps to the pavement before the bus moved off. So, as lightly as she could, she had said to him, "I won't be seeing you again. My job is finished now. I'll be somewhere else, come September."

The odour of melting tarmac through the open door behind her. His face sheened with warmth. Him pushing open the little half-door at his side that was all that kept them apart. Him moving out from behind the wheel. Not a word! She had stepped back, despairing; lost her footing; teetered on the top step and he reached out and held her. Seconds. So close in that confined space.

She had walked away through the bus station sure that he was watching her. She had not known what to do next! She didn't even know his name. And she was ambitious. She had plans to be the headmistress of a primary school. She knew what her mother would say to the notion of a bus driver as a husband. A deadweight. Wouldn't understand what a professional woman needed.

Then one day, that August, she caught a local bus and he was at the wheel. "I swapped with a fella," he said, smiling.

"Sugared almonds!" she said to herself. She had been piqued that when Andy named them on that beach she hadn't known what they were. She was the one with the education, after all. She was the one who was going to educate others. A week later a box of sugared almonds arrived for her in the post. She remembered peeling off its cellophane wrapper, folding back its flimsy lid, parting the paper coverings and seeing those little ovals nestled there. Exactly like the pebbles on the beach. And just as hard. The slight anxiety as she committed her teeth to the bite. The explosive collapse of the shell; the woody contrast of the hidden nut bracing against the rush of sugar.

She had wanted him whatever her mother said about dashed prospects and mis-matching. She had simply known. He was good to the core. And surprisingly passionate in their life together. A man at ease in himself. Instinctive. Not a thinker.

"No ambition!" her mother nagged. But it was, rather, that his ambitions were simple. Go to work. Come home. Do the garden. Be happy. How often his equanimity had tugged her gently back from the brink of some over-reaction. She expected life to be challenging. He met challenges as they arose. When other women shared confidences about domestic troubles – and worse – Mary felt almost ashamed that she had so little to complain of. She was thought to be a good listener.

A sound reached her. A dog barking. A young woman, late teens, walking by the sea; pink jacket and leggings; consulting a mobile, then wrapping her arms around her, head down, another look at the mobile, tucked back under her arm again. A listless walk.

Andy, yes, Andy enjoyed his work. He liked the regularity and he liked the variety. "No two days the same," he'd say. He liked the passengers, especially his regulars, and he rose to the occasional drama. That time, years ago, when a woman had gone into labour on his bus, her waters breaking – he'd announced that he was diverting to the Maternity Unit, no questions; dropped someone at a phone box to ring the hospital; carried her off the bus himself. And when the man with the knife had threatened suicide, Andy had dealt with him. Never once did it seem to occur to Andy that he could opt out. Mary knew that she fussed about the business of authority – having it, wielding it. He took it up, laid it down. Got on with his day.

She saw him before her. "I have been adored," she thought. "*Adored.*"

That final look he had given her as the paramedics took him away. So unlike himself. Wild. Imploring.

And she had let him be taken. No choice. No mercy.

The strange, truncated funeral. Lizzie and Tim not there – Missouri; Dublin. She had manufactured hysteria to ensure they wouldn't risk the contagion of flights. No hugs. Scant. Meagre. Unfitting. There would have been passengers there in any normal time. Staff. Management. Throngs. For her gorgeous, smiling husband.

She looked at her hand, resting on the cold pebbles. Her skin was faintly wrinkled, the eternity ring from Andy sparkling. He had been worried. He had wondered. He had asked about infection risk. The union had spoken up. There was talk of herd immunity.

That was the heart of it. They hadn't been there. No, they hadn't been there – the people who killed him. Passengers. Managers. Shareholders. Councillors. Politicians. The *public*. No protection. A farce. A sham. The truth. The bitter, bitter truth. It coursed through her…. Four times – FOUR times – more likely to die: security guards, shop assistants, construction workers, cabbies, bus-…! Suddenly she was on her back as something hit her, was all over her. She was flailing among the stones. A dog. Barking. Lunging at her head. The girl in the pink jacket shouting at the dog and coming towards her. Something about the curve of the girl's hand, cradling her mobile – did they never, ever stop? Did they never, no matter what happened, stop thinking of themselves first? Selfish. Careless.

Gasping, she tried to get to her feet. The girl was crashing up the slope of pebbles towards her. Mary lashed out at the dog, catching it sharply on the head. She hit it again. It was a very young dog. It cowered. She screamed at the girl. "Get away. Get *away*!" She scrambled up and kicked the dog, hard. It skittered off. Some mutt. The girl's mouth was a shocked O as she lurched backwards amongst the pebbles. "Haven't you heard of social fucking distancing?" Mary yelled. "Selfish little bitch!" She found a heavy white stone and flung it at the girl, wishing her dead. It skimmed the girl's head. Then another. Terrified, the girl scooped the dog up and ran away.

"You killed him. You killed him! People like you!" Mary shouted after her. Mary howled. She howled, more than the dog, more than all the dogs in the world. She dropped to her knees and howled. She dug her fingers into the pebbles and pushed her face into their cold, myriad, uncaring surfaces.

A long time later she was sitting, in the same spot, with her head to her knees, when she heard a slight, thumping crunch among the pebbles to her left. Blearily, she looked across. A large, white stone had landed near her. She leant over. Written on it was the word, 'Sorry' and the outline of a paw. The girl was standing at a distance, awkwardly balanced on the slope of pebbles – poised for flight – biting her lip, looking uncertainly at her. Mary, numb, could think of nothing to do or say. The girl drooped. She turned away and headed back towards where she must have tied the dog up, somewhere along the beach. Mary could hear faint barks. The girl scuffed along the tide line, hands in her pockets, head down. "Oh, God," Mary thought, seeing her. Some weary mechanism began to heave itself to life inside her, painfully. "I have been adored…. Adored." She got to her feet. "Wait!" she called out to the girl.

AMNESTY

"Reverend Coulter, you were born and bred on this estate. As its Church of Ireland rector what does this shocking event tell us about the mood of the people here?" George Coulter opened his mouth. He saw the journalist's professionally alert face, the microphone, the camera. He saw the multi-pointed security fence beyond and, higher again, the supermarket logo, garish against the tentative morning sky and – it was the sky; the sky, struggling to assert itself above the neon with no more in its armoury than the tenderest pink tinge to a pale September wash of blue – it was the sky that did it. The pathetic sky. He gulped and swung away, somehow aware of the journalist's swift gesture to his mate to cut, let it go, for now; the journalist's judicious frown.

Even as he stumbled behind some vans in an instinctive dash for cover he could imagine himself captioned: *Minister Lost For Words*. He wanted to vomit though he felt no nausea; to have some physical pain or punishment, something to stop him thinking. No good. He supported himself with a hand against the cool metal of a van door.

What had made Carson do it? He'd had so much support. People had been protesting on his behalf outside the supermarket for weeks. You couldn't say he hadn't been himself. Being himself was important to a man like Carson. That's how he would have seen the whole business. He'd said what he had a right to say: merely the kind of thing that got said around the Twelfth – though it could never have been innocuous with Carson, convicted murderer of Catholics.

It was, George imagined, a nightmare for the manager, an import from England, a Catholic and, probably, the reason why a co-religionist was taken on in Bakery and one in Butchery. It wasn't so much discrimination that had kept the staff Protestant as the reluctance of Catholics to work in such a hard-line Loyalist area. But times were changing, surely.

It was indeed the Bakery worker who had heard Carson describe the manager as a Lundy, Ulster Loyalism's epitome of a traitor, burnt on the street in effigy every year; the man who would have opened the gates to besieging Catholic forces. How far was someone like Carson likely to take such an analogy?

Had the company turned a blind eye? No. It had applied its procedures and sacked him, though it had not prosecuted. But what the most expensive legal engagement would have been unlikely to achieve, Carson Villiers had managed. The company had re-instated him, 'in the face of popular pressure', as reports (though not the company) had put it. Carson had strolled back into work through applauding crowds and media attention, his return timed to coincide with the manager's arrival.

So why, then? After all that effort. After winning. Why had Carson done it?

George thought of him at the check-out. He was an unlikely-looking till operator with his huge hands scooping up shampoo, dog biscuits, dainties; or reaching over to swing the heaviest things out of the trolley with no visible effort. Good-humoured, Carson had run his till like it was your privilege to pass through his care, like he was dispensing approval or patronage. What a great bishop he'd have made. He used people's names, knowing instinctively who'd be pleased to be called 'Mister'; who'd appreciate a bit of joshing; who actually liked to be dealt with impersonally. George had noted how he nevertheless kept the general area under surveillance: his hands moving across groceries, his eyes sweeping the bigger picture.

Carson, like George, had grown up on the estate. They had gone to primary school together but George had moved on and out, up the educational ladder. It was Carson who knew everything and everyone and remembered everything and everyone. Carson Villiers walked tall, and not only in the Orange parades when the big drum would be strapped to his chest, his shoulders back to support it. How does a man feel, George wondered, marching down his own streets, with the boom of each thud of the sticks pounding through his own body too? It must be like playing your own heart. Is it? You're there at the core of the band, the Big Man, rows of people on either side, cheering, smiling, the weans on people's shoulders, waving the Red, White and Blue.

Amnestied, Carson had walked out of prison in the same way, looking neither to the right nor to the left, his supporters on either side. It was only when he got out of the flashy car that brought him back here to the estate, that he spoke or smiled – so not a few of George's parishioners had reported. Carson had raised his hand, they told George, and they had all waited for him to speak.

"Her Majesty," he said and paused. "Her Majesty is a pretty nice girl and I have been enjoying her hospitality for some years...." This got a laugh, of course. "But, you know what?" he went on. "You know what?" And here he stopped and looked around the entire estate, long and slow. George knew from the way this encompassing gaze was spoken of that people had felt something rare. They had struggled in their various ways to express it. "He knew me," one man had said, "though he didn't. I mean, I was a kid when he went inside but he looked at me like he knew me. He saw me." George was told many times how they felt that Carson, in his steady survey of them, had…. They'd stop at this point but George understood. Carson had taken them on, shouldered them. Things would change. "You know what?" Carson had continued. "Compared to this place, compared to these people, you people and what you have here, compared to what we have here…." Another pause. "Buckingham Palace is shite!" A grin and the place exploded. Talk about a hero's welcome.

That had been years ago. Carson had remained what one might call an activist. He had gone into youth work and it was there they met again. George envied Carson his way with the teenagers. He'd screw up an eye and look at them with the other as though he had all the time in the world, never letting them moan needlessly about anything because he'd say something acute – this man with only a meagre secondary education. He'd take their concern and work it into a plan for action. He was a doer. Yet he'd let the youngster, or whoever, feel it had been their idea in the first place.

George could not compete. He recalled how, the first night that Carson had turned up at the Youth Club, although he had insisted on standing in the background, 'looking on', still the older boys were drawn to him like filings to a magnet. His behaviour was unobtrusive but his presence was unsettling: massively muscled, shaven-headed and mightily tattooed.

Carson altered the balance of everything. He would come, wearing a suit, to 'support the young people' at church parade, or volunteer to drive the minibus on a church outing or swing a mallet putting up a marquee for a fete; he was popular; but George felt himself enough of a clergyman to know that, whatever Carson was committed to, it was not the Lord. Sometimes, George suspected that Carson was making use of God and God's facilities, for his own ends. As long as religion had something to offer Carson's 'brand', it would be enlisted but quietly despised.

George felt this especially whenever he caught Carson's

appraising gaze fixed on him during a sermon. Every weakness of expression, every superficiality, each slip into ingratiating jargon and George would note Carson's discreet, *almost* private, amused censure, as though he were calling into question George's commitment; challenging his record. How far had George been willing to go for his principles, he seemed to imply. Had he walked the walk? Carson had, and however you looked at George's principled return to his roots, he was little more than a dilettante in Carson's view, no matter how many years he put in.

George took to addressing whatever parts of the church Carson was not sitting in and, afterwards, would rebuke himself for such thin-skinned vanity. He recognised that Carson had become what his old pastoral care tutor used to call 'the demon parishioner', the one who puts his finger on you. The more you distrust him, the more you try to compensate with Christian charity but still your distrust grows, so you try harder and your judgement swings more and more out of true, like a maddened pendulum, till you can hardly see your fellow-Christian for the blur.

Carson became a sort of fogged mirror in which George's slightest doubt about salvation or providence was magnified; a silent, knowing critic of assertions about the goodness of God, his smile tolerant of the absurdity of everything George stood for.

Carson's wife, Marnie was the believer, in an undemonstrative way. Marnie McKechnie. Younger than Carson and something of a Loyalist Princess, they had married after Carson's release. She spoke as if her faith was something Carson shared, "We enjoyed that sermon, Reverend. Didn't we, Carson? Took it to heart," she'd say and he'd nod, "Very good, George. Very telling." When Carson shook his hand at such a point, George longed to demand that he come clean, gloves off, and confront him, one hypocrite to another, man to man, if he was so hard. That never happened.

George's wife had reproached him several times recently for his coldness to Carson. She told him he wasn't seeing things in the round but he had responded with flippant aggression, "I've seen you and Marnie, heads together. You hear her confession if you want to. I'll not be rushing to hear Carson's. Our sort of Anglicans don't go in for that. Thank God."

Carson had been heard to say that achieving anything was all a case of knowing where to put the pressure. After certain killings, undertakers had whispered to George about the state of the remains, "Maybe help the bereaved let the viewing go by this time, Reverend." These days it had become rarer for George to be taking funerals. People went to the Evangelicals or the harder Gospel groups.

George didn't know the details of the feuds and positioning and deals among Carson and his associates over the years. The general drift towards a democratic solution for Northern Ireland's problems was clear: the compromises – and the rationalisation of criminality into businesses of a sort. Who'd have imagined Carson Villiers working in a supermarket? But that meant something and nothing. We were all New Men now. And it left time for another life and its opportunities.

So why? Why had he done such a grotesque thing? Why? Why had Carson stood outside the supermarket, doused himself in petrol, set himself alight and walked in front of a car?

It was an inhuman act. And one that had involved others. Four eye-witnesses: two appalled pensioners walking their dogs in the very early morning; the driver, poor man – he had been absolutely traumatised with guilt; and the fourth witness, a parishioner delivering newspapers, who had called George instantly to the scene. George had embraced the driver, repeating to him that he could have done nothing to avoid the collision; that it had been planned and deliberate but the young man, neatly dressed for work in a city office, kept saying: *I could have… I should have… If only I'd….* With Carson's charred body humped on the road in front of them, George wondered angrily what Carson had hoped to achieve by implicating an innocent stranger. The car had been the means to make sure there would be no going back.

Because Carson was thorough, a strategist always. So why no media coverage – if it was a statement of some kind? If Carson had laid down his life, it was for nothing in particular, apparently. He had left a note, though, under a stone by the kerb, asking that George take his funeral.

Christ! George hit the van door with the flat of his hand and was jerked into awareness of the scruffy carpark and of the appalling fact that Carson had implicated him too. He would *not* be manipulated! The church full of Carson's associates; his fans; his widow, Marnie; a eulogy…. No!

All along he had been right to doubt the depth of Carson's 'conversion' to normality. Carson had committed an appalling act. The community needed to recognise the true nature of this hero of theirs. Were they Christians or not? The time had come for him to call the Carsons of this world out. It wasn't too late. Time to put aside scruples about his own worthiness. The Holy Spirit was there for the asking. The Holy Spirit would give him the words to speak, starting with this interview.

He turned just as the journalist approached him, waving away George's apology for needing a moment or two, saying it was natural, a man you knew all your life, a prominent local figure, a community leader, even. "Nasty business," said the journalist.

"I'm ready now," said George.

As they walked back to the storefront George saw that the crowd was growing steadily and he knew what he would say:

Carson Villiers was godless. He executed himself. Ruthlessly. With as little mercy on himself as he had on those whose lives he cut short so brutally in the past. This community thought he was a hero but we don't need heroes like him. Our hero is Christ, who laid down his life, who went to the cross, to save us….

Positioning him once more, the journalist said considerately, "Look, we've already covered the debts and the wife in earlier interviews so we'll just do the community angle with you, Reverend. OK?"

"Debts?"

"Villiers' debts." The journalist's attention was on his iPhone. When George, puzzled, said nothing, he looked up at him as though reminding him of a commonly known fact, "The cross-border fuel scam – Carson trying to go it alone, strung out from the big boys." His eyes back on the screen, he added, "And then, his wife, she was the last straw."

"Marnie?"

"You married them, I believe."

Generations of her true-blue family had been ranged on her side of the church. Classy, by the standards of the estate and always self-possessed, as Marnie came down the aisle that day she had looked wonderful. George saw her before Carson did. He had been trying to avoid Carson's complacent grin as he waited with his best man and it was probably his own instinctive blink of approval that had made Carson turn towards his bride. The naked adoration on Carson's face as Marnie stepped into place at his side! How could he have forgotten that, George wondered. Such vulnerability. Marnie had looked at Carson through the fine mesh of her veil, steadily, then calmly turned towards George. Carson looked only at her.

"She cleared out his bank account – when she ran off."

"What?"

"Yesterday," said the journalist. He suddenly shied back from his phone with a hiss of disgust. "That's a bit strong. Can't see that getting on the six o'clock." He flashed the screen at the cameraman who winced in response.

"Who did she....?" asked George.

"Manager. Look, I've just got to... another witness has turned up. Twitter. Passing motorist. Just let me...." His thumbs flew over the screen.

"With the manager," George repeated. "Of the supermarket."

The journalist nodded, eyes down, engrossed. George reached out and snatched the phone. A figure with its arms stretched wide, a man in flames, stepping off a kerb, a car.... The journalist, protesting, grabbed the phone back and began a call, saying to George, "I'll be with you now." George heard him discuss chasing the supermarket security camera footage.

Of course, Carson would have thought of that. There would be pictures. George reeled from the implications. He put himself in Carson's shoes – in that moment before he'd sparked the irrevocable flame – dripping petrol, choking on fumes, grasping a lighter, about to step off the kerb, and at the click of ignition George was enveloped in a cold flame, furling up around him like a burning flag, showing him.... My God. My God! An abyss. An unfathomable *Why?*

Forsaken, at the kerbside, betrayed and abandoned, Carson had fashioned his own answer: to annihilate himself rather than give his destroyers the last word. He had not believed in the love of God. He had believed in himself, and in Marnie. Carson was a lost soul. George had done nothing to save him yet expected the Holy Spirit to jump to attention the moment he clicked his fingers.

The journalist stowed his phone and posed his question again.

George felt so empty that he could not speak. The journalist, was about to repeat himself but George held up a hand and he subsided attentively. The crowd quietened around them.

George opened his mouth, "Carson Villiers was a child of God. A child who got lost, who didn't believe he had a father to turn to. People like me blocked the light. I didn't show Carson God. I showed him myself. I helped to kill him. Carson challenged my faith in God, and, instead of admitting my weaknesses, I hardened myself to him. May God forgive me and everyone one of us for our blindness to each other's needs. We crucify each other and blame God."

George stopped. He too was lost. The journalist made a cutting gesture to the cameraman and the two exchanged a look that George understood to mean his statement would not be used. The crowd, dissatisfied and uneasy, parted for him.

He walked back to his church numbly, his mind again with Carson, his fingers seeming to clutch that lighter. To have all the love you'd poured out come to nothing, deserted by the one you thought would never leave you, a has-been, a failure.... He stopped, amazed. Didn't he recognise that man? Wasn't that Christ?

He had reached the church. He grasped one of its spear-like railings for he felt the ground giving way beneath him. What was the next step? Where should he put his feet? He was on the verge of something immense.

"Carson", he prayed, "Carson, save me."

"Step out," said Carson. "Is He there?"

ACKNOWLEDGEMENTS

'The Road' was published in *New Welsh Review*; 'Life-Task' was published in *Getting Up*, the anthology of finalists in the Academi Rhys Davies Short Story Competition 2010; 'Snapshot' won the Totally4Women Short Story Competition 2013; 'All Through The Night' was published in *Crannóg* magazine, which nominated it for the Pushcart Prize 2019, and was shortlisted in the Write By The Sea Short Story Competition 2018 alongside both 'Safety First' and 'Coasteering'; 'Above It All' was published in *The Lonely Crowd*; 'Acting Abby' won the Bridgend Writers' Circle Short Story Competition 2017; 'Witness', 'Saint' and 'Saltem' were published in Audio Arcadia's *Eclectic Mix 6*; 'An Ulster Psyche' was published in *Fortnight* magazine; 'The Sea Hospital' was published in *Horla*.

A Literature Wales Writer's Bursary supported by the National Lottery through the Arts Council of Wales was received to develop this collection.

My thanks to publisher, Mick Felton, who patiently refined the collection and to the team at Seren Books for all their work.

Gwen Lloyd Davies, editor of *New Welsh Review*, gave her incomparable editorial attention to the first draft of this collection and set it on its way to further development.

I am especially grateful to Caroline and Patrick McIlroy who, at a key point, gave me a place in which to write; and to Phil Cope who championed my writing and who, with Julian Cason read some early drafts; also to the many friends in Northern Ireland whose hospitality sustained me: Áine Haughey Little, Peter McCann, Rosemary Thomas, Tina and Ian Enlander, RoseAnne and Stephen McCormick, Leigh and Clive Henderson, Marie and Maurice McHenry; and to Jon Gower, Laura Foakes, Damian Smyth, Dr Sharon Jones, Angeline King, Graham Reid and Kate Hamer for their particular support.

And my thanks to the very many people who encouraged and helped me; most of all to my husband, John Geraint and my children, Róisín, Anwen and Seán.

AUTHOR NOTE

Angela Graham is from Belfast. Before writing *A City Burning* she was a TV producer and director and a feature film screenwriter in Wales, making over 100 documentaries and factual programmes for BBC, ITV, S4C and Channel 4. She was also Development Producer on the landmark BBC series and double BAFTA Cymru-winner *The Story of Wales*. She produced and co-wrote the Welsh/Irish cinema feature *Branwen* (Oscars entrant in the Foreign-language category and winner of international awards) and was the screenwriter of feature film scripts set in Italy and Romania.

Her stories have been widely published and praised for their virtuoso handling of tone and voice. Graham is a Welsh-speaker and award-winning poet.